VAMPIRE WARS

THE LONGEST NIGHT

Heather Knox

EPIC Escape

An Imprint of EPIC Press
abdopublishing.com

The Longest Night
Vampire Wars: Book #3

abdopublishing.com

Published by EPIC Press, a division of ABDO, PO Box 398166, Minneapolis, Minnesota 55439. Copyright © 2019 by Abdo Consulting Group, Inc. International copyrights reserved in all countries. No part of this book may be reproduced in any form without written permission from the publisher. Escape™ is a trademark and logo of EPIC Press.

Printed in the United States of America, North Mankato, Minnesota.

052018
092018

Cover design by Candice Keimig
Images for cover and interior art obtained from iStockphoto.com
Edited by Jennifer Skogen

Library of Congress Cataloging-in-Publication Data

Library of Congress Control Number: 2018932897

Publisher's Cataloging in Publication Data

Names: Knox, Heather, author.
Title: The longest night/ by Heather Knox
Description: Minneapolis, MN : EPIC Press, 2019 | Series: Vampire wars; #3
Summary: In an attempt to thwart the Praedari's kidnapping of another captive, Delilah finds in Zeke's killer an unlikely ally—and a myth made manifest. With the Valkyrie's help, Delilah finds herself nabbed by the Praedari, only to realize she's been here before. Kiley learns from her what fate awaits them all at Project Harvest, and Anonymous declares war on the Everlasting.
Identifiers: ISBN 9781680769067 (lib. bdg.) | ISBN 9781680769340 (ebook)
Subjects: LCSH: Vampires--Fiction. | War--Fiction--Fiction. | Kidnapping--Fiction--Fiction. | Delayed memory--Fiction | Young adult fiction.
Classification: DDC [FIC]--dc23

For Sylvia Quinn

"I'M GLAD YOU DECIDED TO GET CHECKED OUT BY OUR
doctor, Logan—though I apologize that with
all the commotion surrounding our most recent
arrival he wasn't able to pay a visit to your suite,"
Victor says, offering a small, sympathetic smile. He
waves to Hunter and Kiley. Hunter makes a show
of unpacking in the suite as the doors close behind
Logan and Victor with their trademark whoosh.

Once in the hallway, Logan shrugs. "I play football
so it's worth making sure no real damage was done,"
he responds, just as Kiley coached him.

"Well, if you find you're craving a workout during

recovery—and the doctor clears it—maybe you could pitch in around the ranch. It would get you some escorted outside time. I'd have to find adequate security for you, but I'm sure it could be arranged."

"During the day?" Logan asks, a bit more eagerly than he'd like. "I mean, because you're all . . . you know . . ."

Victor chuckles. "Sure. We'd start you on a night team so I could be around—for your safety—but there are plenty of mortals who work here at all times of the day." He pauses. "Our staff is compensated quite well for their nontraditional living situation—and many others are volunteers. I know it'll probably be difficult for the three of you for a while, being thrust into this without your consent, but there really is a place for you here if you give it a shot."

Right, Logan thinks. *As dinner.* But he keeps his thoughts to himself as Victor escorts him down the corridors leading to the infirmary. In this part of the facility the floors gleam almost too-white in the fluorescent lighting, clinical, emphasizing the bright silvery-steel of the doors they pass. Quiet, besides the sound of doors like the one to their suite sliding open with a soft, metallic whoosh and the occasional click of shoes on the tile somewhere out of sight. Quiet, besides his breathing and Victor's attempts at friendly chatter that Logan finds difficult to respond to without animosity, opting for the occasional grunt and half-hearted nod. Quiet, besides muscle memory— that crash of fear in the chest as he was run off the road by fanged strangers just the night before and abducted—screaming at him to run, just run.

Victor looks to him expectantly as they stop in front of a set of polished, nearly seamless steel doors, much like the others but with a touchscreen, digital numerical keypad, and full digital keyboard. In addition to its various inputs, the apparatus boasts an impressive array of scanners—the retina one like for entry into their suite, what could be a fingerprint ID, places to both swipe and tap an ID card, and other scanners Logan can't identify the purpose of.

"Fancy," he comments gruffly, gesturing to the console.

"Some of the equipment the medical team has requested for research is quite expensive—we're talking beyond what the military has access to, very privatized and highly controversial—but when Doctor Larkin stipulated it as a condition of his employment during contract negotiations I found it hard to say no. Others fought it, but I insisted," he explains into the retina scanner after punching in a sequence of characters on the digital keyboard that Logan couldn't catch.

"Because he's the best?"

"That, and because the research he's doing is important. For us, and for you. But here we are." He grins as a set of heavy steel doors slides open, not with a soft whoosh but with a series of beeps, revealing a second set. Another console, boasting the same inputs and scanners as the first, lights up with the face of an older gentleman. This man has salt-and-pepper hair (more salt than pepper) and his hazel eyes are alight. There's a flush to his cheeks as though he'd just rushed in from the outdoors and to the console to greet them. He breathes heavily between exclamations.

"Victor, my boy!" he greets them with surprising warmth. "Is this my patient?"

"Sure is. Doctor Larkin, this is Logan. He got a bit banged up by the extraction team."

"Ah, yes! Their handiwork will make sure I earn my salary this quarter it seems!"

"Sorry, doc," Victor apologizes, running his hand through his short hair, brow furrowed.

"Nothing to be sorry for—this is why you hired me!"

"Still, it's not your job to clean up their messes . . . How *is* Charlotte, by the way?"

The old man on the screen waves away Victor's polite protests with a smile. "She's stable. Remarkable, really. I'll send you the full report, of course." He pauses, studying Logan through the video screen. "His leg, I take it? And his back, by the looks of it."

"Yeah, how did you—" Logan starts but Doctor Larkin interrupts. He still walks gingerly, though most of this charade served to get him here to see Charlotte—but never, not even to Kiley and Hunter, had he mentioned his back bothering him after the accident.

"The way you're standing, son. You're lopsided. Now, some people are just lopsided but not most. You've got good bones, I can see, so you're not usually lopsided, are ya? Are ya, son? Lopsided, I mean?"

Logan involuntarily stands upright in response, raising an eyebrow at Victor who coughs to stifle a laugh. "Uh, no. No sir, I'm not usually . . . lopsided."

The old man takes a half-step away from the monitor and looks behind him a moment before addressing Logan and Victor once again in the screen. "Anyway, come on in. Looks like the, uh, little mess we made patching Charlotte up is all taken care of. Medicine can be a sticky business!" He laughs at his own attempt at a joke. "Now Victor, you know the rule."

Victor holds his hands up in faux surrender.

"Wouldn't dream of breaking it, Doctor. I'm just his escort. Call me when you're finished with him."

"No vampires in my infirmary," he explains, Logan presumes for his benefit. "Can't heal an undead patient . . . " He laughs again, shaking his head. "I tried. It was a disaster."

Victor shrugs at Logan before turning again down the corridor from which they'd come. He turns his attention again to the screen as the doctor clears his throat.

"Come in, come in," he says waving his hand as one might at a child you're trying to get out the door after it took them twenty minutes to put on their shoes. "Don't got all day, son. Girly here's coming to but I can squeeze you in. She's rough . . . real rough," he adds with a grin.

The doors open and Doctor Larkin meets him, guiding him hurriedly by the shoulder inside.

"Put up a good fight, that one did," he says gesturing to a girl in her teens lying on one of the beds, eyes closed. The slow, steady rise and fall of her chest confirms to Logan that at least she lives despite how washed out she looks underneath the harsh lighting of the infirmary—sickly against the blond of her hair, still matted with blood.

"How 'bout you? That how you got hurt?"

"Eh, not as much," Logan admits, ashamed, unable to look away from her. "They ran my car off the road and I got banged up in the accident. What happened to her?"

"Gunshots to the abdomen, stomach, chest. Bad, real bad."

He guides Logan to a bed in the adjoining room to that of the girl, not bothering to draw the curtains despite the observation window.

"Alright, drop 'em."

"What?"

"Your pants, drop 'em. Can't look at your knee if I can't see it."

"Uh, right," Logan says, unzipping his jeans and letting them slip from his waist to his ankles.

"If you're shy you shoulda wore shorts, son. She's

groggy, won't remember past the blood haze. Don't worry."

The doctor cups Logan's heel in his hand, gently pushing and pulling his leg to test his range of motion.

"Blood haze?"

"Poor girl'd be dead if I didn't have all these corpses walking around with their super-blood pumping in their veins. That hurt?" he says, jabbing a bony finger into the soft flesh behind the kneecap. Logan winces. "Guess so," he laughs. "Anyway, that IV," he gestures to the tube attached at the inside of the girl's elbow, through which Logan now notices red liquid rather than clear flowing there. "It's going in, not out—and that's not medicine."

"So you're turning her into a vampire?" Logan demands, eyes wide.

"You've seen too many movies, son. A little vampire blood won't make you one. That bag is diluted, of course, a custom blend of vampire blood and human blood of her blood type. That blood has allowed her body to regenerate almost as well as one of these corpses could." He beams up at Logan as he knocks him on the knee evoking a solid kick in reflex. Logan grunts. "Wasn't sure it would work, truth be told—but she made incredible strides dayside."

"Dayside?"

"During the day—keep up, son."

"You experimented on her?" Logan asks, vowing to not miss a beat after the reprimand.

"It's not like it's a shade of lipstick on a monkey or pumping rats full o' saccharine. Victor asked me to save her life, so I did."

"So she's going to be okay?"

"You sure ask a lot of questions," he says, standing and turning to one of the cabinets.

"I, uh, well—" Logan fumbles.

Doctor Larkin returns to his side, knee brace and tan cloth in hand. He waves away Logan's failed attempt at speech. "Save it. I would, too, if I were you. She'll be fine. Better than fine, for a while, no telling how long. Then she'll be normal again.

Straighten your leg." He slips the tan bandage-sock over Logan's calf up to his knee.

"So whose blood did you give her? Victor's?"

Doctor Larkin jostles Logan's leg as he adjusts the brace, the sound of Velcro punctuating Logan's question.

"Just some blood from the bank," he shrugs, patting Logan's knee hard enough to make him scowl a moment. "Good as new! Well, you will be. Just keep that on for a bit when you're walking around. You can take it off to sleep and to ice it. Your profile said you're an athlete?"

Logan nods.

"Then you probably know how to R.I.C.E, right? Rest, ice, compress, elevate? Shoulda had you come in right away, but anyway, ice it for about twenty minutes every hour or two until this time tomorrow. Walk around a bit when you're not icing it, ibuprofen for the slight swelling. You'll be fine, just some jarred tissue from the impact. Of course, we could speed it

15

up . . . " The doctor's gaze shifts to Charlotte in her bed, a sparkle in his eye.

Logan follows the doctor's gaze to the girl, tube in her arm transferring the red of their captors into her veins. On the metal surgical tray on the table next to her bed a package of clean bandages and a fresh spool of tape waits. Nearby, the small red bin marked *Biohazard* struggles to contain the mound of white-and-red that threatens to spill over. He wonders how many similar packages she bled through, how quickly, and how much of that blood was hers? How much of what's inside her is hers?

"I'll stick with ice," he responds with a shudder, wondering if the girl would have given consent—or if it would have mattered.

The doctor sighs. "A pity. I'll have Victor bring you by tomorrow night so I can take another look at the bruising." He guides Logan to the first set of doors and punches some keys—the last few numbers he recognizes as being the number Victor gave them to contact him with their tablets or the in-room com system. "Who knows? Maybe Sleeping Beauty here will be better company then."

Before

*E*ZEKIEL THE *SEEKER*.

The honorific rings in my ears, resonating through the tightly-woven network of my veins, nearly electric. My beast sniffs at the shift within, snorts in disgust, in warning, nostrils flaring. This predator-self has no use for these shackles of status we impose upon it: a custom of the Keepers shunned by the Praedari for this reason. My title, bestowed by the Council of Keepers centuries ago—amazing how inconsequential a millennium-old tradition can appear to the outsider when stripped of its ceremony. Those of us who've earned such a title have grown weary of the burden, our albatross we bear until we are ash—and longer, for the truly unlucky. Memory haunts relentlessly.

The woman standing before me in the otherwise abandoned alley Victor and his men just left, holding sword and shield, makes no movement, yet I feel her presence swell to fill the void of the nearly-abandoned alley—a predator, but not of a type that my inner Beast recognizes, smelling faintly of the floral-sweet taint of some of the luckier Everlasting, but also of freshly-fallen snow. Where I expect this shadow-self to stalk and snarl and lunge as when met with danger, it instead sniffs and remains vigilant out of respect to the unknown, uncertain whether to show submission or dominance because neither me nor my shadow-self know which hierarchy should be the yardstick for measure.

Both her glow and that of the moon refract in the sword and shield which sometimes pulses to glow as she does, but also threatens to drip like molten metal, though their texture this close reveals wood grain for hilt, blade, and shield alike. She wears her red hair pulled away from her face in something like braids, but loose and messy in the back. With sharp features and full lips, I hesitate to call her beautiful; no, striking fits better, of similar stature as Delilah and with that same confidence. In another life she may have ruled an empire.

"Who're you?" I demand again.

"I will not answer a question you full well know the answer to. To do so would demean both of us. I am here to offer you a choice, Seeker," she says evenly.

The forgotten black bird caws before swooping in low from the dumpster, landing on the shoulder of the woman.

"You're—"

The raven. The sword and shield. The way she stands, erect and untouchable, as if from not only another time, but another world.

"You may choose to continue living or you may choose to meet your Final Moment and allow me to bear you to Valhalla where the Chosen of the Slain await Ragnarok," she interrupts.

"I did not think the Valkyries offered a choice," I begin. "And this dirty alley is hardly a battlefield."

She shrugs. "Times change and so must we. The Praedari see this, embrace this. The Keepers, though—you cling to tradition, often to the detriment of your cause, but such blind stubbornness can be attractive. Can be useful." She gestures around her. "Looks can be deceiving, Seeker. This was once a battlefield—and will be once again."

"Why am I being offered a choice?"

"As I said, we've been watching you a long time. We are not opinion-less, though we refuse to be distracted by involvement in your war. Tell me," she starts, cocking her head, "how would we choose from amongst the slain if no one died in battle? How would we find those *einherjar*, those warriors honorable enough and skilled enough to join us for the one, true battle at Vigrith—during Ragnarok, the Twilight of the Gods—if you did not fight here for something?"

"So it is true, that the Valkyries prepare for Ragnarok?"

She rolls her eyes and sighs, the first time her stoic countenance stumbles. "All of Asgard prepares—and has been since the beginning of time. Those warriors not worthy of Valhalla join Freya at Folkvangr—look, this is far more complicated than I have time to get into with you right now. I gave you your choice. Now make it." Her jaw sets in a hard line, unwavering despite the earlier crack in the figurative mask she must bear as one of the Choosers of the Slain.

"The Keepers and the Praedari prepare for a war that has been gathering momentum for centuries," I explain.

"And you are being offered this choice now. You think you have set the war between your sects in motion, but you have not. The Everlasting will hold their courts, will wither away and rot in their beds of inaction—"

"You speak like you are not one of us."

"I am a Valkyrie. A long time ago I was one of the

Everlasting but now I am something more. And I'm giving you the chance to become something more than what they've made you. If you refuse us now you may return to the night to await your battle and, should you fall, you may find yourself offered the hand of a Valkyrie again." She steps towards me, her hand on the hilt of her sword but still. "But it is not often one of the Everlasting is offered a place in Valhalla, and it has never happened twice," she warns.

She pauses for a second that stretches into too many, herself stretching to become moonlight and stardust and shadow—to become past and present and future, the known and unknown at once. "It is time for you to die, Ezekiel Winter. You may join me now and take your place among the honored dead in Valhalla, or you may die forgotten. You have glimpsed the future through your Oracle. You know I speak the truth. You know what is to come."

"And what of my Oracle?"

"She, too, will be offered a choice—but her fate is not yours."

3

Now

Nᴏᴛ ꜰᴀʀ ꜰʀᴏᴍ Dᴏɴᴜᴛ Eᴍᴘᴏʀɪᴜᴍ, I ᴄᴀᴛᴄʜ ᴛʜᴇɪʀ scent long before I hear the commotion. The predator within me howls and I am caught off-guard, a sound I haven't heard in the hollows of my body since my first time hunting with the Praedari pack Zeke and I infiltrated—a sound I manage to prevent my throat from echoing in this moment by clenching my jaw. Instead, a whimper escapes my lips, a paltry impersonation of what rattles inside me and causes the hairs on my body to stand at attention. Whether I've entered someone's territory or they've entered mine is uncertain, arbitrary, as neither the

Praedari nor the Keepers claim this strip as their own and no individual holds territory successfully without acknowledgment from their sect—regardless, a predator is a predator and mine aches for a fight.

Commendable, the strength of those Praedari choosing to live as a pack, their Beast-selves learning to not only exist alongside one another but to hunt and thrive as a cohesive unit. Years of intensive training allow most Keepers to mingle with Everlasting other than their own Usher with whom they share blood, but even then our inner Beast only retreats for a while, allowing us to swallow the dark urges calling to us from deep within our psyches, chipping away at the delicate armor we've erected in an attempt to deny this part of ourselves. But the Praedari do not deny this second nature, do not require rigorous training to control the predator within and do not suffer the same way as a result. Keepers pay the high cost of denying this dual nature when they finally snap. In that we pose the greatest danger to ourselves and to our cause.

Tonight, three distinct scents, each like a fingerprint, unique in subtle ways but always bearing the taint of one of the Everlasting; likely a Praedari pack hunting. Were they but passing through, the night would not betray them. No, they've been in the area long enough to saturate the streets with their stink. I haven't faced a Praedari since the last of our host pack fell. I wonder if I could pass as one of them now.

Then the commotion: shattering of glass, screams, gunfire.

"How do you even say her name?" Johnny asks his packmates with a sneer. "More-gawks?"

"Come now, poppet, is that what you call customer service?" Pierce asks with a pout as he looks first to his bullet-riddled chest and then at the girl who stares at the three of them down the barrel of a handgun which trembles in her grasp. Her eyes wide, her dark brown visor now slid back and dangling from her ponytail as she backs towards the rear exit. "Trigger-happy twit . . . " he mutters.

"No wonder no one claims this litterbox of a

territory—even the donut girl is packing heat," Lydia announces as she steps through the now-shattered front window. "Can't even get an easy meal . . ." she laments to no one in particular.

Johnny hops over the counter to stand in front of rows of metal trays of donuts. He raises his hand to cup his chin in exaggerated consideration.

"What are you in the mood for, Lyd? A blueberry cobbler croissant donut? Butternut? Apple and spice? Maybe you want something filled with a little red . . ."

With that he grabs a jelly donut from the tray and stuffs it in his mouth, crumbs erupting from between his lips as he laughs. A glob of jelly oozes out of the end of the pastry and lands on the stubble covering his chin. In an instant he's inhaled two glazed and half a butternut, the sugary fallout coating his palms, fingers sticky.

In another instant red spews from between his lips as he wretches, covering the counter with blood and undigested donut chunks. Pierce glares at Johnny as the girl huddles with her back now against the wall, chamber empty but still she squeezes the trigger rhythmically, as if in a trance.

"Gross, Johnny! It's like *The Exorcist* up in here!" Lydia screeches in disgust from the relative safety of the illuminated storefront window cavity.

"Worth . . . it . . . " he manages from between spastic, wet heaves.

In another instant the girl slumps against the wall, hitting the dingy off-white tile with a sickening thud.

5

Now

"**D**ON'T TELL ME TO CALM DOWN!" HUNTER shouts, fists balled at his sides, face shifting from red to a sort of purple. "They're pumping her full of vampire blood and we're supposed to sit here waiting for them to—to what? To let us go? To eat us? To turn us into one of *them*?"

"I'm tellin' you . . . she looked a lot better. I'm not saying I agree—"

The crash of wood-meeting-tile as a nightstand hits the floor interrupts Logan, the drawer yawning and spewing forth its contents: a notepad, a pen, a couple bottles of pills.

"Dude, *chill!*" Kiley demands as a pill bottle rolls to her feet. She kicks it towards Hunter who stands amidst the immediate debris just a few feet away. The contents clatter to the floor, tiny orbs of pink and green and blue.

"Chill?" Hunter takes a couple long strides towards her, drawing back one fist.

Logan steps between them. Where his normally stockier build would typically dwarf Hunter's slender frame, the latter, bolstered by his rage, seems nearly as large—and easily twice as reckless.

The first punch Hunter throws glances off Logan's neck, pitching Hunter's center of gravity too far forward. Logan puffs out his chest in anticipation, letting his shoulder catch Hunter in the jaw with a snap as his upper and lower teeth come together too hard. Logan shoves Hunter, sending him toppling backwards to the floor.

"Stop!" Kiley screams, but the two don't seem to notice.

Logan takes a few steps towards Hunter who

clamors to his feet and takes a step back, hands up in front of him in surrender. As Logan lunges, Kiley launches herself onto his back, wrapping her legs around his waist and one arm around his neck.

"I said *stop!*" she yells again as she starts pummeling Logan's head with her clenched fist—more desperate in her flailing than exerting any real strength. "I. Don't. Need. To. Be. Saved!" she yells, each word punctuated by a rap on Logan's skull.

"What the—?!" Logan spins around a few times, trying to loosen her grip on him.

Hunter, now backed against a wall of the suite, starts laughing—at first quietly, then crescendoing to a deep belly laugh that has him doubled over. Kiley's assault slows, her clenched fist now relaxed and its attached arm joins her other around Logan's neck to hold herself on her non-consensual piggy-back ride.

"What're you laughing at?" she demands.

"You! You're . . . he's . . . with your . . . " Hunter imitates her flailing. "I don't need to be saved!" He manages between laugh-choking breaths, flailing again.

"Shut up!" she yells, stifling her own laughter and twisting in an attempt to get Logan to put her down. "Let me go!"

"No way!" he laughs, clamping her legs with his arms. "I've got her—get her diary!" he calls to Hunter.

"Don't you dare!" she yells, resuming her flailing on the back of a chuckling Logan. She yanks his hair and he tries to cry out, but the sound is swallowed by his own laughter.

Hunter scrambles for her bed, reaching under her pillow. He pulls out her black hardcover Moleskine journal and flips it open, reading aloud.

"'Things that kill them: sunlight, garlic?' 'Crosses' is crossed out . . . 'Ash when dead like on *Buffy*?'" Hunter rifles through a few pages, pausing a couple seconds on each to scan the contents. "'Get Lydia's story,'" he continues. "'To Interview: Victor, Lydia, British guy, thug guy, others?' Are these . . . notes?"

Logan releases his hold on Kiley, letting her drop

down. She lunges for Hunter and the journal, swiping it from his hands.

"Obviously! What else would it be?" she hisses, clutching the journal to her chest and glaring at the two boys. "How is that even a question?" she mutters under her breath.

"Kiley, do you really think that interviewing the people who kidnapped us is going to accomplish anything?" Logan asks, the concern in his voice mirrored in his gaze.

Hunter scoffs. "She probably thinks she'll be the next Anne Rice once we get out of here," he mocks. "*If* we get out of here," he adds, returning her glare.

"Actually," she announces, "I have a plan."

Now

I AM JUST BLOCKS FROM THE ALLEY WHERE ZEKE DIED when I hear the glass shatter—alone, not something I'm too concerned with in this neighborhood, but when gunshots erupt into the otherwise quiet night I feel as though the breath I no longer draw has been knocked from me. I remember the girl working at Donut Emporium from a few nights ago, firearm tucked into the small of her back and covered by her polo, not hidden but out of sight.

Zeke called episodes like these omens—not quite a vision but a feeling, my predator within responding to something unseen or, in some instances, something that has not quite come to pass. When feeling optimistic, I call them impressions; more often than not, I call them distractions—what good in knowing there will be a tornado but not where it might strike?

Tonight, though, I heed my inner Beast, knowing it likely a pack of Praedari are on the hunt. I jog towards the sound and, sure enough, the sidewalk in front of the illuminated windowfront of the Donut Emporium glitters with glass shards. A quick survey reveals the front counter covered in sticky red and a single whiff of the metallic tang tells me what I need to know: they were here and, judging by the quantity of blood, got what they came for. I turn and dart to the end of the building, ducking into the narrow passage leading to the alley.

I press my back against the exposed brick of the wall, cool and rough on my flesh. Hushed voices quarrel, punctuated by whimpers muffled by something soft. I lean forward to peer around the corner: near an unmarked dark blue van, a man—large in build, almost Herculean even from this distance—covered in blood hoists a squirming young woman over his shoulder, bound at the ankles and wrists with zip ties and gagged half-heartedly with something tied loosely around her jaw.

"I don't see why I can't have a taste. I'm hungry." He speaks to someone I can't see and the van's engine roars to life, headlights bathing the dumpster in bright. The dark color of the captive's shirt makes it impossible to gauge the extent of her blood loss, but if the mess inside is any indicator, it's a miracle she has this much fight left in her—unless this pack recruits rather than hunts this night.

"That's because of the digestive pyrotechnics *you* thought would be *so* incredibly funny—" a voice from inside the van retorts.

"It was!" The large man guffaws, obviously amused with some earlier shenanigans that the unseen person references.

I sniff: the familiar stink that awoke my predator within to howling is now overbearing. Three distinct scents, the same I've been tracking, but also something else, at once familiar and new, Everlasting and not. The girl? Did they forgo their barbaric Rite of Becoming, turning her here? Are the Praedari that desperate for numbers that they'd neglect their savage customs? Unable to rely on my sense of smell, I try to see if the girl is breathing. If she is breathing, she is still human. But I can't tell if her chest rises because she is squirming too much.

Hidden from sight by the dumpster, I don't see her until she has already called her packmates' attention to me—another young woman, no older than the one slung over her packmate's shoulder, dressed in torn jeans and a dark T-shirt that probably boasted some band but the screenprint has long since crumbled. Her hair's pulled on top of her head in a messy knot, wisps of it having fallen out of place now framing her face. She brandishes a long hunting knife with a devilish grin, popping a bubble of her gum as she takes a few measured strides in my direction. I feel that dark part of myself start to swell, filling me in response to being discovered. I swallow it down, save for a growl that escapes my throat.

"And what have we here?" she asks, sniffing. "A pretty little Keeper so far from home? And what's that?" She sniffs again. "She brought a friend along to play?"

A second man steps from the van, leaving the door agape, and makes his way towards her with a casual gait. As soon as I catch his eye I find myself, for a moment, unable to look away: one eye a medium brownish-red, the color of a red fox's fur, and the other bright blue, the effect startling against the dark of his skin. I glance around the alley, counting their distance to me in the reduced seconds of an Everlasting's reflexes. I step into the alley, away from the corner I'd been tucked behind, planting my feet firmly to meet them. I cross my arms over my chest, gaze unflinching.

"Manners, Lydia. You don't know she's a Keeper," he rebukes. "But she *is* right—you are lovely," he adds with a thick accent and charming warmth, smiling at me.

"Quit flirting, Pierce," his packmate volleys, rolling her eyes.

Behind them, their sneering packmate busies himself with loading the squirming, bound woman into the cargo area of the van, seeming to struggle with not knocking her head or limbs against the vehicle. The awkward way he tosses her around, nearly dropping her more than once and in quick succession, leads me to believe he's not usually the careful one of the three.

"What's with the precious cargo?" I demand, indicating the captive with a quick shift of my eyes.

That's when I see shadow flicker underneath the van, cast from the far side, unnoticed by the man nearest it who's finally wrestled the captive into the van with some muttered cussing—unnoticed, too, by the two whose attention I have. From my peripheral vision I see the large, black bird from the other night perched on the dumpster.

She brought a friend along to play? the young

woman had taunted when she discovered me. I caught the scent of the three of them and someone else— but what if the someone else wasn't the girl they'd come for?

That's when I realize there's something else here besides me and them.

S OME SAY WHEN WE LET OUR INNER BEAST TAKE OVER
we allow our ancestors in. For those Elders still
alive—or Slumbering—we allow them to see through
our eyes, to feel through our touch. We honor them,
but in doing so we become vulnerable to them, more
than one tale told of an Everlasting unable to recover
from the bloodlust of their ancestors that sang in their
veins.

Most Keepers dismiss this as nonsense, but the
Praedari live it, building elaborate rites around the
idea of honoring one's ancestors by embracing the
predator within. Their Ritus Essendi, the Rite of

Becoming, demonstrates the ultimate in submission to one's ancestors: from the outside looking in, they succumb entirely to their bestial-self in a moment of desperation, scrambling to survive and, in doing so, proving themselves to their sect.

In truth, they channel the strength of their ancestors. The scramble to survive allows their Elders to move through them, to be one with the earth again, to relive their own Becoming and honor their own ancestors, and so forth. Even those that fail to climb from the dirt to be reborn experience this connection with their ancestors and serve the sect in doing so. Those Elders in the Slumber experience through them their own Becoming, something the Praedari believe vital to keeping them loyal to the sect even as the passage of time may have otherwise jaded them to the cause.

Politics aside, there's beauty in this, that we may live again in those we created—that we may, in those we created, and in ourselves, summon those who've gone before. In this way we are never truly alone.

In this way none of us ever truly dies. Our Final Moment becomes just another moment of many.

The Prayer of Ascension

FROM THE RITUS ESSENDI OF THE PRAEDARI:

O Blood of our Blood

and Blood of Before,

all the way back to our Mother:

we gather as Brothers and Sisters in noctis,

stars underneath Her moon,

to light the darkness

for those we buried.

O Blood of our Blood

and Blood of Before,

the Longest Night has come.

Theirs is not a mass grave,
but a shared womb.
Theirs is not to die,
but to be reborn.

And we shall receive them
as they Become,
O Blood of our Blood
and Blood of Before,
cradle them to our bosom,
guide them in the Eternal Hunt.
Amen.

Now

MY INNER BEAST SNARLS AS I SNARL, FANGS EMERG-
ing as I subconsciously step aside and unleash
this part of me for what might come. This is not the
Keeper way, allowing the predator within to guide
rather than lurk denied underneath the surface. No,
this I learned while infiltrating their ranks. To defeat
them I must, for now, become like them, unhindered
by emotion and logic. In a way it feels good to let go,
to step aside and allow myself to be someone else,
some*thing* else. To allow those with whom I share
Blood to sing their ancient wisdom through my

actions—the secret to the predator within that the Praedari know and the Keepers will never.

The girl notices the shift in me before the others, lunging for me blade-first before I can offer the first strike to catch them unaware. I snarl again and lunge in her direction, our bodies crashing against one another. I manage to narrowly avoid the blade itself as it slices the air just centimeters from the delicate flesh where my earlobe meets my neck.

From the rear of the dark blue van I hear a low, vulgar whistle as I grab Lydia's wrist and wrench her knife-wielding arm behind her back with a twist. Johnny slams the cargo doors of the van, leering.

"Who *are* you?!" she growls.

"Chick fight!" the large, ugly man admires. He's taken up a baseball bat, the handle whittled down to a sharp point, and tosses it from left hand to right and back as he approaches with a sneer. "Come on Pierce—we may be dead but we're not *dead*, if you know what I mean . . . " Despite his lewd words, I can almost hear his inner Beast snarl as I manhandle his packmate.

"We *always* know what you mean, Johnny," Pierce says, rolling his eyes. He eyes his helpless packmate with concern but makes no move to help her.

I yank the knife from her caught hand, eliciting a sharp kick that would have shattered a human's tibia but instead meets mine—sharp pain but no lasting damage. She reaches her free hand behind her and grabs my hair with a hard yank.

"I wouldn't do that if I were you, gorgeous," Pierce warns. "Lydia doesn't like people touching her things." He takes a few steps towards us.

"A little help, guys?" she hisses.

"Oh, so now you need help," he mocks in an almost brotherly way, putting his hands out in front of him in mock-surrender. "I seem to recall a lengthy lecture just last week about how you're more than capable of handling yourself and—"

I barely have time to pull back so I can gather the momentum needed to plunge her knife into her ribcage from the side when someone catches my arm at the elbow.

"Hey now," Pierce continues, now at my side, standing close enough I feel the chill of his skin nearly touching mine. I turn my head to gape at him in surprise. He holds my arm hard enough to cause bruises to bloom. "I'm trying to have a discussion with my packmate that you're rather rudely interr—"

Once recovered from the stun of his speed—greater than any Everlasting I've traded blows with—I release Lydia's arm and spin on Pierce, flicking my wrist to toss aside the knife which hits the pavement with a clatter, and punching him below the belt, hard, with a tightly clenched fist. He grunts as I connect. Some things hurt no matter how immortal you are. Lydia stifles a laugh as her packmate drops to his knees, eyes wide. *I, against my brothers. I and my brothers against my cousins. I and my brothers and my cousins against the world*—truer for none than for the Praedari.

That's when I notice her: a statuesque woman

with sharp features and red hair that seems to reflect the moonlight. At her hip, a sword in its scabbard; strapped to her back by a few thick ribbons of leather that cross above and underneath her breasts, framing them, rests a shield. The index finger of one hand rests on her lips as she takes careful steps behind and towards Johnny; in her other hand a sharpened scrap of wood but gleaming black. Or is it shadow? I blink in shock—where did she come from?—my predator within faltering a moment, allowing me to swallow instinct down and carry out this fight myself, unaided for the moment by the ancestral bestial cunning of a berserker in the throes of battle.

My being distracted offers Lydia a chance to snatch up her knife and take a defensive stance next to her now-staggering packmate, both facing me, unaware of the precarious situation Johnny unwittingly finds himself in. I see the woman's arm draw back, away from her plea for my silence, as she moves the other to clench a long shaft of wood or shadow by both hands.

The rest unfolds in slow motion, in an eerie

simultaneity. Pierce growls and rushes me—still staggering and halfway hunched over—but my attention remains fixed on Johnny as the woman deftly plunges the length of the makeshift wooden stake into his back and out his chest. His cry rises into the night, quickly building to a loud, wet gurgle, causing Lydia to turn his way as Pierce succeeds in tackling me to the ground. We crash to the pavement in a tangle of limbs, jaws snapping at the other—not a puppy's playful nips but two killers looking for blood.

"Johnny! Noooooooo!" she screams as she takes a few running strides towards her skewered packmate.

Pierce leaps off me to join her. Both stop mid-stride as shadow envelopes Johnny from behind, where the woman once stood and from where she launched her covert assault—though they never saw her, only the thing bursting through his chest with a spray of blood. In an instant nothing stands before them save for a shrinking pool of flickering shadow on the pavement which, too, dissipates. I am left to imagine the pile of ash that should have been, the pile of ash all Everlasting leave for their allies to mourn and their enemies to spit upon. In a cruel twist of fate it seems Johnny's pack will not be given even that.

With the nothingness that lingers nearly palpable, I use the distraction to scramble towards the van, keeping to the shadows and making sure I'm not seen. They shout after him as though his name alone could conjure him from the darkness, could bid him return from his Final Moment—a reaction I know all too well and for a moment my own grief over my own loss threatens to rise up and seize control, a familiar heaviness in my limbs as my eyes sting with tears. The choke of a sob forms in my chest, at once a boulder and a hole.

As they scan the alley, hackles raised, I climb unnoticed into the driver's seat, slam the door, and peal backwards, screeching in the opposite direction they survey. Through the windshield I see them shouting and giving chase, see Pierce fling himself at the hood of the van, hear him near-miss as he bounces off with a thud, see him roll noiselessly on the pavement behind me.

I do them a favor, leaving them to their grief.

10

Before

LYDIA WATCHES AS AURELIE—EVERY BIT AS DELICATE as her name, every bit as delicate as their Usher—slides like silk from the settee, her feet not making a sound as they land on the marble of the floor of her penthouse suite.

"It's barely past sunset," Lydia pouts, wrapping a throw blanket around herself.

"Mistress needs me," Aurelie explains, slipping on an ivory cardigan. Against the light fabric, her dark locks fall in stark contrast, grazing her waist.

Lydia rolls her eyes. It irritates her that Aurelie would call their Usher that after so many years; the girl's years far outnumbering her own. She looks on as Aurelie plaits her hair into a loose mermaid-style braid, wondering what she sees in the vanity mirror. Were she mortal, would she be dust? Putrid, worm-eaten flesh? Something else?

"Don't be jealous, *mon petit oiseau.* This target requires . . . finesse." She sets the antique metal brush down on the marble vanity, the expected clink lost to Aurelie's Gift of Silence. Her reflection frowns at Lydia through the mirror.

Aurelie inherited not their Usher's gift, but instead blossomed to become her own: silent as the sunlight that was her namesake, but far deadlier. Truly the only gift like it in the world; the most prized of their Usher's collection.

"You mean she doesn't trust me," Lydia challenges, her voice taking on the edge of a predator whose territory is being threatened. Indeed, that within her slinks nearer the surface, a phantom flush warming her skin. She lets the blanket drop to the floor as she stands, stretching and crossing to the window overlooking the city. A welcome chill rolls off the glass.

Below, traffic drags itself through the falling snow, muffled by a flurry, the street entirely swallowed in white. She always thought the winter beautiful, even when she was between homes. Perhaps that's why she found herself so comfortable with Aurelie: the silence. She never asked how Lydia came to their Usher's fang and she returned the favor in kind.

Lydia startles as fingertips graze her skin, sweeping a few stray hairs off the nape of her neck.

"Hush, now," the woman whispers into her ear. "You know she trusts you. Where is this coming from?"

Mon petit oiseau. My little bird. The nickname rings in the hollows of Lydia's ears, the innocuous phrase—indeed, a common term of endearment in French—morphing to carry a bile Lydia could nearly taste, a bile something within her could. She'd first come across the words in a letter, written long ago in the scrawling, even handwriting of their Usher and kept in the girl's copy of Baudelaire's *Les Fleurs du Mal*. She'd happened upon it when Aurelie was called away on another of their Usher's tasks and it had sparked a fight. Their first and only fight after they became friends. Temperance loved Aurelie best, the letter made that much clear, and still she sent her prized assassin after dangerous targets to settle petty, ancient grudges. Didn't she care she might lose her?

Aurelie holds her arms out to Lydia—a peace offering. Lydia turns slowly, stepping just slightly forward, closing what little gap remains between them. She wraps her arms around her friend.

"Goodbye," Lydia whispers into Aurelie's ear.

The room falls silent, even the sounds of the traffic below quelled as Aurelie's blood gurgles from her throat and pools on the floor. Lydia needn't see to know how wide Aurelie's eyes were as she's drained of life. Tears wet the cheeks of both women.

Better my fangs in her neck than another consuming her Heartsblood. A mercy kill.

For a moment, everything exists as if in a mirror:

the pooling blood and the dull gray of the knit throw blanket. Then ash, her sunlight lost.

11

Now

I AM JUST OUT OF THE ALLEY, STILL GUNNING IT IN reverse in the opposite direction of Lydia and Pierce, when I glance in my rearview mirror. I am only just able to slam on the brakes to avoid hitting the figure I see there. Within seconds the passenger door opens and the red-haired woman from earlier hops into the seat as if invited.

"Well met," she says brightly as the door slams behind her.

"What the—"

"Drive!" she orders, adjusting the scabbard at her

hip as one might a seatbelt, as if it were the most normal thing she could possibly be doing.

"Not until—"

"Delilah, drive," she orders again, this time her voice more stern than excited. "Those two aren't going to find their ashed packmate any time soon and they're out for blood now. Soon these streets will be crawling with Praedari."

"'Well met,' alright," I mutter, shifting into drive and slipping my foot to the right to depress the gas pedal evenly. "The enemy of my enemy is my friend," I sigh to myself without thinking.

"I'm not the enemy here, Delilah," the woman says, offering a smile. "But I know who you think is— even though you're not quite sure yourself, anymore, are you?" I glare at the road, a proxy for her. "Who the enemy *is* is rarely clear—and always subjective— but I can take you to their nest if you wish. You can find out for yourself if you're right."

Nest. Not many Everlasting use that term, as it's considered vulgar—as in, a rodent or insect nest.

Something you want to get rid of, a nuisance. It's fallen out of use by the Keepers because the word itself evokes the idea of a problem to be solved, something to be disposed of—something capable of becoming a threat if left too long—and they left the problem of the Praedari far too long. The Praedari never preferred the term out of pride: nothing that "nests" rules from the top of its food chain.

"Hands on the dash where I can see them," I demand, knowing full well that had she wanted to kill me she'd just have done to me what she did Johnny. What *did* she do to Johnny?

She leans forward with a smirk, placing her hands on the dash. That's when I catch her reflection in the passenger-side mirror, the same reflection I saw in the broken vanity mirror in the alley the other night as I retraced Zeke's final moments. Was she there? Did she follow me?

"You see my reflection as I am, and yet you wonder *what* I am," she muses. "You wonder if what you see is what I see, if I, too, am cursed as you. And if I am not, why?"

"How do you know my name? Why were you back there?" The questions tumble from my lips before I can stop myself. I add, in an attempt to recover a sense of being in control, "This is unclaimed territory, belonging to neither the Keepers nor the Praedari, and rarely do either risk traveling through it."

"I knew your Usher," she offers without really answering. "I was there because I knew you would be. You've been digging, looking for the one who killed your beloved."

"Who are you?" I ask, voice edged in threat.

"I am the one who killed Ezekiel Winter."

◈

"*What* did you just say?" I demand. A knot in my stomach forms, surges past my ribs up into my chest cavity where once my heart beat and continues to press up into my throat. I don't need to breathe, but I couldn't if I tried.

"I said, 'My name is Quinn' . . . " She cocks her head to the side as if to study me. "But that's not what you heard, is it, Oracle?"

My knuckles turn chalk-white as I clench the steering wheel. My jaw aches with the effort of choking off the Beast within, my top and bottom molars grinding into one another to form the blockade. I swallow down bloody bile, the urge to vomit nearly as great as the urge to tear out this woman's throat with my teeth.

Since I offer no response, she sits back in the seat and continues. "The Seeker had been searching for us for a long time. Longer than you've been one of the Everlasting and nearly as long as he had been."

"Choose your words carefully . . . " I warn from clenched jaw.

"I know well your lineage, Oracle—Childe of Ezekiel the Seeker, Grandchilde of Ismae the Bloody—and I know well the carnage you are capable of, even if you are not. What I offer now is the truth, nothing more. It is rare we get involved in the dealings of the Keepers or the Praedari—"

"We?"

Her gaze remains steady, never leaving the road. "Turn left here. There's a safe house where we can drop the girl."

The girl. I'd forgotten about her. No telling what injuries she's sustained or what emotional state we'd open those doors to find her in, but I take some comfort in learning that Quinn wishes to keep her safe as I do, even if my desire has taken second-fiddle to knocking together some Praedari skulls. Though we have an obligation to protect humanity, Keepers aren't perfect, either. Duty at odds with desire, it's rare the former wins out. With little reason not to, I follow her instructions, turning down the street. We've edged closer to Keeper territory, at least.

"A Keeper safe house out here?" Often the Keepers would erect safe houses in or near enemy territory for operatives infiltrating to have access to. Some the

Keepers maintained, with high-tech security, blood stores for emergencies, caches of weaponry for both offensive and defensive maneuvers, and the means to take one's own life if one's identity and affiliation were compromised. Most of these safe houses were derelict, having been ransacked by the Praedari or locals or just crumbling from disuse and neglect.

She shakes her head. "As I said, we rarely get involved in the dealings of either sect—nor do we rely on their efficacy, or lack thereof. This is a Valkyrie safe house, operated by my sisters. Once we leave, your memory of having visited it will fade until it is nothing—a precaution, of course, nothing personal."

I glare at the road. So much of what I've been through, who I am has been lost to the Becoming. Whenever Zeke would tell the story of how we met, of how he came to choose me for the rite, it would echo as distantly familiar only to be swallowed up by sunrise. For some reason nothing stuck unless I dug it up myself—and it seemed that my mortal me had a reason to make sure nothing *could* be dug up about her.

"You are not pleased," Quinn states, interrupting the silence.

"I do not like my mind being messed with. By anyone."

"I understand," she says in a soft tone that makes me want to believe her. "I know you've lost a lot to memory, perhaps more than you know. But you will discover all of this in time."

"You know I have visions," I state, choosing my words carefully so they cannot be dodged. "You referred to me as the Oracle, but the Council of Keepers has not honored me with a title as per our custom."

She smiles. "You are correct—they haven't. *Yet*. Others have. All will unfold in time, of course," she says with a sigh, "but your Usher understood why he had to make a choice *now*. I hope you, too, will come to understand what is being asked of you. For now, don't worry—no one will invade your privacy. The magic is in the place, not those within."

Now

"SHE'S *HEAVY*, FOR BEING SO OLD," LIAM COMPLAINS, his fingers and palms rubbing raw from where they struggle to support the bottom of the cement burial vault. "She can't be that big, right?"

The vault: roughly seven foot by three, cement-re-inforced with steel rebar, wrapped in heavy chains. A vault of utility, not vanity, the cement dull gray and not polished to gleaming, the coarseness of medi-um-grit sandpaper. The weight not beyond what Liam alone could carry, such the blessing of their Blood, but Victor instructed them to be careful, that though Ismae Slumbers in a coffin within the vault, she's, as he put it, "precious cargo."

"Come now, brother, surely it's not all bad," Mina teases from the other end of the vault, smiling as they both shuffle underneath the weight and importance of what they carry. "You've turned the head of nearly every woman we've passed, and most of the men."

Liam laughs, glancing down at his own shirtless chest, the fine sheen of sweat broken out over his skin and the runes there, carved into his flesh post-mortem as he hovered between the worlds of the Living and the Dead, in the tradition of their family Bloodline. The muscles of his chest and arms bulge, no longer the lean muscle of a predator giving chase, but transformed into the savage beauty of the predator tearing into his kill. His sister's strength nearly matching his own, he notices her silhouette likewise transformed but to lesser degree, another trick of their Blood.

He doesn't bother obscuring his strength the way she does, but then he's not burdened with the double standard of beauty that women are: be strong but not too strong. He's lost count of how many idiots have fallen to his sister's fang, too distracted by the threat they perceive in him that they underestimate her. Her Keeper-kills probably out-tally his own, but it's a good tactic for them, tried and true.

Why take another packmate when they have each other?

Now

"**Y**OU SHOULD TELL HIM," PIERCE SUGGESTS, NUDG-
ing Lydia in the ribs as they trudge up to the
ranch house.

Her packmate's tone catches her by surprise, lower
and softer than she's grown accustomed to from him,
so she nods. The wooden, weather-worn welcome sign
on the door ahead knocks in the wind. Though she
sees it daily, and has for the better part of a year, she
hasn't noticed it until now—how the dark knots look
like bullet holes from this distance, even with her keen
vision; how the bark along the edges has flaked where
the warp in the wood forces contact with the door on

windy nights like this; how many rings in the slice of trunk, each indicating another year of weather, of disappointment, of mistakes, of surviving. Somehow the paint has endured, faded of course, but still legible, in the handwriting of someone likely long since dead.

"Wait . . . " She shakes her head, her voice catching in her throat so she clears it. "Why me?"

"Victor likes you better," he offers, opening the door for her.

As she passes him, her arm brushes his chest. He grabs her roughly and pulls her against him in a tight hug. She tenses a moment, then wraps her arms around him. A tear slips down her cheek before being absorbed by his shirt. The hug lasts only a fraction of a minute but it feels as if it could be years before Pierce's hands move to her shoulders and he pushes her away from him to look at her. He wipes a rogue tear from her skin.

"Don't cry in front of them," he warns as a father might. "Bite it back. I'll wait up for you in our quarters and you can weep until sunrise, if that is how you choose to mourn."

She nods, both surprised by his understanding and not, such illustrating the delicate balance between competitor and caretaker that living as a pack requires.

"And the Rite of Mourning?"

"Soon. Neither of us will feel up to hosting the rite until we've had a chance to mourn privately—Victor will understand this."

" . . . and the girl?"

"Well, that's where you work your magic, Little One," he says with a sigh, falling back on a nickname he gave her when they first packed. Though it started as condescending and derisive, it fell out of use for a while before becoming a term of endearment he only used with her in private, out of earshot of even Johnny. "He may well choose to bring us to the tanks after we've mourned for failing our mission—in which case, tonight might be our last night together."

"Got it," she says with a sharp nod of acceptance.

She barely makes it completely in the doorway when Victor spots her and waves, giving an expectant smile. She glances behind her but Pierce has slipped back out into the night to avoid him.

"Lydia! I'm glad you're back, I was getting worried. Where are the others?" He looks around for emphasis, not asking the question burning in his throat like bile: Where is the girl, the fifth descendant of Ismae the Bloody?

"Pierce slipped out for a minute," she starts. And there she stops, unsure of how to continue. "Victor . . . Johnny didn't . . ."

"What is it, Lydia?" His brow furrows as he studies her, arms crossing over his chest.

"The girl got away," she starts again, this time focusing on a different narrative.

"Got away?"

"There was another woman there, one of the Everlasting—she fought like a Praedari . . ."

"What do you mean 'she fought like a Praedari'?"

"I mean she wasn't a Praedari but she *fought* like

one," she tries to explain, finding it much easier to focus on that woman and the lost girl than on the loss her pack must now endure. So she babbles, unable to stop herself for several minutes as she recounts the night, every detail she can recall in case something they thought inconsequential ignites a spark of recognition in their leader—but his expression remains a non-expression, unreadable.

"And Johnny?" he asks as she pauses, having reached in her account of the night the very thing she subconsciously sought to avoid mentioning, as if by not mentioning it to an outsider she and Pierce could forget, could resurrect their fallen packmate.

She shakes her head no, looking down at her bloodstained Converse. *Do not cry*, she repeats in her head several times, filling the silence between them such that she cannot move nor speak aloud.

"I'm not angry," he states.

"You're not?" She looks up at him, mouth hanging slightly agape in disbelief.

"Well, I am . . . " he admits. "But the girl is unharmed?"

Lydia nods.

"And you didn't go after them?"

She hesitates only a moment before shaking her head.

"Good. If the Keepers are on to us they may have led you to an ambush."

He reaches out and squeezes her shoulder.

"You look as though I'm going to turn into a giant snake and swallow you," he says with an unconvincing tight-lipped smile. While that exact thought hadn't crossed her mind, now she can't erase the image. "We learn from failure. In this case, we've learned we're on the Keepers' radar—probably someone poking around for information about Ezekiel Winter's involvement, or his death. We don't know how much they know, but we know they know something."

"But the other pack—" but she is silenced by Victor holding up a hand to cut her off.

"The other pack were idiots and almost killed their

intended target. Their entire pack was almost brought down by a little girl and a crazy old farmer. You," he pauses for emphasis and squeezes her shoulder again before letting his arm fall to his side. "You did nothing wrong. You exercised good judgment and should not be punished for that."

"We could go after her again," she offers, but he shakes his head.

"If the Keepers are on to us, it's only a matter of time before they put the pieces together. You'd either be walking into an ambush or forcing their hand—which might compromise the girl's life. They won't kill her when they can hold her up for us to drool over. No, this moves up our timeline—but it's not a crisis."

"Do you need her to awaken Ismae?"

He shrugs. "I don't think so—the blood of the four should establish a strong enough connection to this plane to bring her out of her Slumber to the waking world."

"And if it doesn't?"

He considers this a moment. "First things first: go rest. If it doesn't work, I might need you and Pierce again. I would join you in mourning, but I promised one of the kids a tour," he adds with a sigh.

As she retreats down the hall to the quarters shared by her pack to rejoin Pierce, a familiar tightness wells up in her chest, blooming to her extremities which now tingle. She balls her fists. How dare he send them after some girl he might not even need? How *dare* he send them to do his errands like hired help, like they're expendable? Is this what Johnny lost his life over, a maybe? A shaft of wood through his heart because of a misstep by Victor? Victor, whom they follow without question, whose ambition to raise the mother of the Praedari has blinded him to the movements of their enemy. Too distracted, unable to see the forest for the trees. Now Johnny would never again see the forest nor the trees, nor the fruit of their toil here at the ranch, would never see the Praedari take their rightful place as predators, stamping out the Keepers' antiquated notion of nobility—and for what?

She wheels around but Victor has gone. A guttural sound builds in her stomach and surges from her throat, turning to a scream that fills the now-empty hallway as the predator within climbs up and threatens to follow the path of her voice out. She turns to the wall and puts her fist through some paneling with a sickening crack of the bones in her hand as they fracture, sending sharp tendrils of pain up her forearm. The tears that stream down her cheek stream not because of the pain, but in an attempt to drown out the rage that summons her Beast within.

Don't let them see you cry.

14

Sometime in the '80s

"AND DON'T LET THEM SEE YOU CRY," THE GIRL with the curls and too much mismatched concealer caked over bruises warns. She wears a nice skirt, and her red heels—a size too big and scuffed with the black of asphalt—match the red of her flawless manicure.

Lydia nods, wiping away tears with her sleeve. The room smells like bleach and jasmine, the carpet so covered in stains that the coloration—shades of yellow, beige, and brown—would look intentional if it weren't so disgusting. She hadn't caught the girl's name, but she suspected that the omission was intentional. Lydia had heard that the woman who runs this house treated the girls like slaves—sending them out to cook and clean for wealthy families in exchange for a place to stay. They were supposed to dress nicely, though, so they would reflect well upon their mistress.

"Hush now, don't scare the girl," a low, sweet voice from the doorway admonishes. "You're going to be late for your appointment, and you know we don't tolerate tardiness."

The girl with the curls blushes and looks down, nodding, shuffling from the room.

"Now that we're alone, what's your name, girl?"

"L—Lydia."

The woman frowns. "That won't do. Lydia is too boring. I like to give the girls more interesting names—call yourself Lolita, Lola if they're regulars. It'll make them feel closer to you when you are cleaning their houses, scrubbing their toilets. Help them to trust you. We do it for the money—but secrets are the real currency."

We—as if this woman had ever, in any other life, found herself three weeks without food that hadn't come from a dumpster. Instead, Lydia asks: "Lolita?"

She narrows her eyes at Lydia, studying her before continuing. "You're not much of a reader, are you? Tell me, how old are you?"

"Eighteen, ma'am."

"No, you're not," she states not accusingly, but knowingly, as she leans against the doorframe, crossing one ankle over the other and her arms over her chest.

"I—I'm fourteen."

"Ah, no wonder you haven't read it. No matter, really," she says with a wave. "I have a copy you can borrow."

Lydia continues to sit quietly, staring at the woman in the doorway, absorbing every detail about her: the cloud of Chanel No. 5 surrounding her like a far-reaching halo, probably from the same type of crystal-cut glass bottle as the one her foster mother received as a gift that she accidentally broke (and was forced to lap up like a dog, two homes ago); the diamond earrings that dangle halfway down her throat and look remarkably like a pair a foster sister stole (and accused her of stealing—she still has the scar on the back of her hip where the belt tore open her flesh and the earrings weren't even real); the nakedness of her left ring finger, a "most vulnerable" nakedness Lydia's last social worker warned her would be her fate if she ended up behind bars (and, likely, even if she didn't).

But the way this woman wore that nothing was nothing like the way Lydia's mousy social worker wore it, as a self-deprecating badge of honor as she constantly frowned and constantly found herself late to their check-ins, scrambling as if she owed the universe a great debt that she'd never quite settle.

"You're different," the woman announces, standing straight. "Follow me."

Lydia jolts upright from slouching and follows, scooping up her backpack—mostly empty, save for an empty plastic water bottle, some metro tokens she stole, a few photos, a few dollars, some socks, and a stuffed knit owl in a plastic baggy. She'd never say she had nothing. *How long have I been staring?*

The woman leads her down a series of hallways of the condemned hotel, dirty low-pile carpet in dark olive green and orange worn to the floor in well-trafficked areas, littered with twitching and glassy-eyed junkies whom the woman steps carefully over. If the building had been kept up it would be gorgeous; with the revitalization of surrounding neighborhoods, Lydia figures it's only a matter of time until it is demolished, displacing those that struggle within, herself now among them. She scurries to keep up, tripping on the foot of one and catching herself on the sticky wall. A grumble. She apologizes. The person attached to the foot doesn't respond, instead staring past her at a chunk of peeling wallpaper, floral and cream.

The suite the woman steps into requires a keycard and smells of autumn: cinnamon and falling leaves. This scent is so far removed from the putrescence of the rest of the building that Lydia finds it diffi-cult to catch her breath. It's clear she's kept this suite as an office: a desk and leather desk chair, a coffee table and settee, a modestly-sized wardrobe of ornate wood. Above the desk, monitors show security camera footage from around the building, entrances of some private rooms—with a few exceptions, including the room they just left—the timestamp indicating the present.

The woman lets the door click shut behind them, noticing Lydia's stunned expression. "My office—I own the building, and others like it, just haven't had the heart to disrupt the lives of those who've been here longer than I. Please, sit," she offers, indicat-ing the settee. "Or perhaps you'd rather shower and change?" She wrinkles her nose at Lydia, the question more a command than a suggestion. "The bathroom is through there, use whatever you need. I'll find some clothing and leave it by the sink."

Lydia shuffles to the windowless bathroom with her backpack and closes the door behind her without a word. She runs the water, drops her clothes into the small trashcan underneath the counter with a swish-thud, and steps into the first shower she's had in weeks. As the water washes over her, she lets her tears mingle with the droplets but doesn't sob aloud. *You're different,* the woman had said and no part of Lydia wants to find out what this means for her here. She wishes she could melt into the water and be washed down the drain. Maybe she could find the ocean. She can't swim, but anything would be better than here.

The door clicking shut startles her. She pokes her head out of the shower curtain to find freshly deposited clothes on the counter, as promised, and a towel spread on the tile in front of the tub. She lets the water hit her face a few moments longer before turning it off and stepping out, wrapping herself in a towel. She takes her time dressing, first slathering herself in lotion from an expensive-looking bottle. She dresses in the clothes left for her: a soft romper boasting a geometric pattern of jeweltone pinks and reds and purples and a similarly hued cardigan. She spots a set of goldtone bangle bracelets and a pair of boho-chic amethyst earrings meant for her next to the pile, but leaves them by the sink. Instead of the nude heels left for her, she pulls a clean pair of socks from her backpack and slips her boots back on. A cream color and not yet dingy, she had stolen them from a charity thrift shop last week. A frequent "customer," she's sure the staff there knows she's stealing but haven't the heart to bust her for it. In return, she brings donations of things she's rescued but has no use for. Not really an even trade, but she doesn't take advantage of their kindness, grabbing things only as she needs them. She hastily pins her hair back in bobby pins before collecting her backpack and rejoining her hostess in the suite.

"Oh good, it fits," the woman claps with a smile. "I wasn't sure your style, but these colors look great on you."

Lydia notices her eyes linger first on her bare wrists and then her boots, but the woman says nothing, just continues looking pleased with herself.

"Come, sit." Lydia finds herself obeying. "I'm sure you have questions—"

Lydia shakes her head. "No, ma'am—I'm ready to work." Despite the confidence of her words, she swallows loudly the lump that's formed in her throat.

The woman offers a fake pout. "Call me Temperance, please. Ma'am makes me feel old," she says, laughing softly.

"Okay."

"Lydia, this place—this life—this isn't what you were meant for. Now," she puts her hands up in fake surrender, "I admit that I don't know what you've been through or why you're here. And I'd never ask. But I know *people*—"

"Please," Lydia starts to implore before realizing the desperation in her voice. She didn't need to be saved from herself. "Please let me work. You won't be disappointed. I'm a fast learner—"

The woman holds up her hand to stop her.

"I'm not telling you no, child—but I *am* offering you a choice. You can leave here tonight as Lolita, if you wish. You would stay with the other girls who spend their days mopping floors and scrubbing dirty pots till their fingers bleed. Or . . . you can remain Lydia, and be mine."

"What do you mean?" She squirms a little in her seat. She doesn't like the idea of being owned.

Temperance takes a seat on the settee next to Lydia and leans in. "I'm offering you a chance to leave all of this behind—but everything as you know it will change."

Lydia considers whether Temperance means to offer her entry into some sort of pyramid scheme, but she's also sure that Temperance wouldn't be so stupid as to think she had any kind of collateral to offer as down payment. Perhaps this woman recruits for a cult? Needs to hire a drug mule? Harvests organs for the black market? None of these seem too dire a proposal to turn down without at least hearing her out, at least as compared to her present situation, so Lydia listens.

"You're a . . . a vampire?" the girl in front of Temperance asks, cocking her head to one side. Temperance recognized potential: Lydia would make a great killer. Innocence becomes her.

"One of the Everlasting, yes. Vampire is such an ugly word." Temperance has removed her heels and drawn her legs up, leaning on one hip with her long legs stretched out to her side and her arm, bent at the elbow, resting along the top of the settee. She looks as though she stepped out from a painting found in an ancient temple a long time ago, that same wisdom and grace emanating from her form.

"And I'd be one of them, too?"

Temperance nods.

"Will it hurt?"

"Only for a second."

"And then?"

"Most find it enjoyable beyond measure. Though occasionally that is not the case," she admits.

"I mean, then what? I'm a vampire and then what?"

Temperance smiles at this, amused by the thought the girl puts into the decision, albeit almost certainly a ruse to make her seem less desperate. Still, the move shows calculation, a discerning nature even if for show, something she can appreciate. Especially of a fourteen-year-old girl. Such potential.

"And then you will be in my tutelage for a number of years—not alone, of course, as I have Ushered others whom you will join. I will provide for you and teach you the ways of our kind and, in exchange, you can help me with things. If you want," she offers with a slight shrug.

"What things?" Lydia's eyes narrow.

"I have a number of business dealings that require different types of finesse—as I get to know you, I'll get to know your strengths and interests. If you are a whiz with numbers, maybe you'll help me with accounts. If you're a brawler, maybe you'll act as my bodyguard from time to time. If you want to leave, you can. I'm not offering you a job, Lydia—I'm offering you a family. This isn't about what you can do for me in the future; it's about what you can do for yourself right now."

"Why me? Did you make this same offer to the other girls?"

"No. And I won't. I noticed you studying me—you're different, sharp. You're *worthy* of the Blood."

"Sounds a little Third Reich to me . . . "

She smiles. "See? That wit. You're bright and quick. Tell me, how many steps from here to the door?"

"Fourteen." The answer fills the space between them nearly as Temperance finishes the question. So easy to coax forth.

"What color was the shirt of the man you stumbled on in the hall?"

"Dark blue and gray with silver—Dallas Cowboys.

A hole at the collar on the left side about the size of a quarter."

"You're an eidetiker." *And a survivor,* Temperance thinks. *And really, what choice do you have? What choice do I have? My collection needs an eidetiker.*

It's not that Temperance is wrong about Lydia's photographic memory, but despite the gifted programs her social worker pushed her families to enroll her in, none were willing to foot the bill or do the extra driving or attend the additional parents' programming. After all, she was already another mouth to feed, why waste the meager board payments on her education? Her eidetic memory was something she learned to keep private, a weapon no one could see. It wasn't that she dumbed herself down the way she noticed other girls her age sometimes would; no, she merely saw benefit in not showing her cards until she'd already won the hand.

"What will it be? Shall I call you Lydia or Lolita?" the woman nudges. She could use the gifts of her Blood to coax from the girl the answer she wants, could ply the girl using the Gifts of her Blood, but what's the fun in that? Half of the thrill is the chase. She's grown so bored of her other playthings that she bought out this rat-infested pit of a hotel just to have something new to do.

"What of the others?" Lydia asks.

She shakes her head. "Believe it or not, there are rules even I have to follow. None of the Everlasting offer this choice lightly. Think of it in terms of population control: what happens when too many predators are introduced to an area?"

"Food becomes scarce." The same goes for the streets and every week, it seems to Temperance, the fight grows more vicious for less and less reward. She'd known girls in this position before, between families and vying for resources—she wasn't one for paranoia, but there seemed something swelling underneath the city, a momentum pushing more and more urchin like Lydia to be swallowed up by it, to be lost forever. At least this way she could teach the girl to push back.

Lydia bites her lip. Her voice fills with resolve. "Call me Lydia."

15

Now

"**I** WANT TO GET A MESSAGE OUT," HUNTER SAYS, clunking an empty glass on the nightstand next to where he's been examining the tablet in his hands for the past hour and a half. "It's all currently wired to an intranet, but it's capable of doing more if we hacked it . . . "

"Do you know how?" Logan asks from where he lies on his back on the floor, a pillow propping up his head and his foot resting on a chair.

"Not even a clue."

"Great," Logan rolls his eyes.

"Guess I'll stick to floor-plan duty," Hunter sighs,

the tablet crashing onto the nightstand next to the bed he's claimed as he drops it next to the glass. The other two wince. He turns his attention to Kiley. "Have you talked to the girl vampire yet?"

"Lydia? The one who we've been eavesdropping on for the past several minutes? The one whose name has been said no fewer than thirty times *tonight*?" she challenges, pacing and chewing on her thumbnail as she scowls.

"Yeah, her."

"We're all stuck in this room together—have you *seen* me talk to her? I did convince Victor to give her access to us, though."

"When?"

"Whenever she wants it."

"No, I mean when did you talk to him?"

"While you were staring at that tablet trying to go all Neo on it." She stoops to talk to Logan in an exaggerated whisper. "Is he *really* the one we want mentally mapping the facility? I chatted with Victor for no fewer than ten minutes."

"About pie. I remember," Logan teases with a smile. "What was that about?"

She shrugs. "You don't watch many political dramas, do you? People love to talk about themselves. Besides, I got us the promise of pie, didn't I?" She matches Logan's smile, finding it hard not to.

Hunter mutters something under his breath and joins Kiley in pacing, back and forth and back, when a scream from the hallway stops him. He glances to Logan and Kiley, and then to the door.

"Was that—?"

"Definitely a girl," Logan finishes Hunter's sentence, sitting upright and sliding his injured leg off the chair.

"Lydia?" Kiley jumps up from her crouched position to listen again at the door, but she hears no voices.

She and Logan had been successful enough at listening through the door moments earlier to glean that Lydia's pack had returned from some task Victor asked of them, likely to do with the missing guest, but then Lydia spoke too low and muffled for them to hear much more so Logan gave up to stare at Hunter staring at the tablet, grumbling about needing to elevate his leg.

"Lydia! Lydia what's wrong?!" Kiley yells at the door, pounding to get the girl's attention.

The door slides open just as Kiley's fist would make contact, knocking her off balance. Her fist glances off Lydia's shoulder.

"You're going to wake the entire facility," she admonishes, stepping inside. The doors slide shut behind her.

"You're vampires. It's nighttime," Hunter quips.

"Alright, you got me there," Lydia says, irritated. "But our staff is human. And tired. Now *what* is going on?"

"We heard you scream," Logan explains.

"And?" Lydia barks.

Logan and Hunter step back two paces before turning and heading to their shared kitchenette. Kiley catches the slight nod Logan gives her before focusing again on Lydia.

"Something wrong? You seem . . . tense."

"Yeah. Look, now's not a good time to braid each other's hair and play Ya-Ya Sisterhood . . . "

Kiley's voice drops to a whisper. "The guys didn't hear your conversation with Victor, but I did. Most of it."

"So?" Lydia shrugs. From the kitchen the girls hear cabinets banging shut and the guys laughing about something.

"Come on. Your eyes are puffy and red," she changes her approach when she sees Lydia's hands ball into fists at her sides, avoiding mentioning Johnny altogether. "All I'm saying is that you helped make my transition here a little smoother. Let me return the favor. Let me listen. Who else do you have to talk to?"

"I don't need to talk. I need to kill her!"

Something hits the kitchen floor with a wet thud, the sound followed by the guys laughing again.

"I know! I know," Kiley consoles. "But for now

you're on security detail. Cabin fever is real. *I've almost plucked out Hunter's eyes a dozen times tonight and—*" she raises her voice for his benefit. "I *swear* if he slams another *anything* I'm going to." She lowers it again. "Look, I doubt it's going away just because you're grieving. Do you really want to lash out at your sadistic British friend right now? Or Victor?"

Lydia eyes her suspiciously, so Kiley rushes to continue. "What else am I doing? The guys get field trips and I get to sit here watching reruns of *The Real Housewives of No One Really Cares*—maybe you can tell me more about being a vampire. For my research. You *did* promise me interviews."

"Fine. Tomorrow night," Lydia manages through a clenched jaw after a long pause. "We'll talk and I'll let you know who'll spill their guts for your family newsletter or whatever."

Hunter emerges from the kitchenette crunching on something. Logan follows.

"You—" Lydia points at Logan. "You and the new

girl are starting yard duty with Liam and Mina once she's up. Victor said you mentioned getting outside, wanted to see if you were up to it yet."

Logan nods, leaning against the doorframe leading into the kitchen.

"Who're Liam and Mina?"

"Vampires," Lydia answers flatly.

"Hey. You giving me the tour tonight or what?" Hunter asks between bites.

"Do I look like a freakin' concierge? Victor'll take you when he has time to babysit," Lydia snarls. "By the way, he was out in the yard when that little fight earlier broke out, but he saw the camera footage of it. He says the next time that happens he'll come here *himself* to break it up."

With that, she spins and storms from the suite. The door slides shut and Logan counts to ten under his breath before speaking.

"Think she bought it?"

Kiley nods. "I'd feel worse about it if we weren't hostages."

"Bought what?" Hunter challenges. "Your grand plan is to befriend one of the vampires who helped bring us here and hope she, what, has a change of heart and lets us out? Tells us about some service entrance not covered in my tour?"

"You need to chill," Kiley warns.

"It's not a great plan, but it's still a plan," Logan interjects. "The more angles we work this from the better our chances of getting out of here. Since we still have no idea why we're here, getting Lydia to talk might be our only way to get more information. I mean, who else do we have? Victor isn't going to talk and the doctor is straight-up crazy."

"The crazy one might have some insight," Kiley offers. "Keep talking to him. And it sounds like maybe that Charlie girl will be awake soon."

Logan gives a nod of agreement. "Can't hurt to bolster our numbers, right?"

Kiley turns her attention again to her verbal sparring match with Hunter. "This plan costs us literally nothing to try. Zero risk, and we might piece together enough details to learn why we're here or how we can get out."

"No risk, no reward," Hunter counters, letting a second empty glass clank on his nightstand. Kiley glares.

"You take all the risk you want," Kiley says, flopping onto her bed. "See how long until one of them sinks their fangs into your neck."

Now

QUINN LEADS ME THROUGH A COFFEE SHOP PAST MISmatched couches of three different vintage orange-and-green floral patterns, reminiscent of the '70s, and one of olive green crushed velvet. Each host to tables from vastly different eras—mid-century modern, someone's garage sale a few decades ago, an Amish woodworker a year ago—and various low-slung faux-leather chair seating, some corners of seating finished with aquariums and all punctuated by years-old coffee rings. Retro diner, office, and elementary school chairs in various states of disrepair—some glittery blue vinyl, some a sickening aqua or yellow metal, all with quasi-threadbare cushions—scatter around two-person tables painted with cribbage and chess boards, their pieces occupying small wooden boxes on the bookshelf that boasts a smattering of abandoned books and board games whose missing pieces have been replaced by customer-made variants. No two lamps, nor their shades, so much as complement one another and, in that, the entire place glows with a homey warmth.

Along the eastern exposed brick wall of the original architecture, local artists—likely long since passed through this area—have displayed their work. Despite the eclectic assortment, all seem curated with a semi-industrial aesthetic: stormtroopers join a Victorian family for a black-and-white portrait, Darth Vader assuming the role of father and sitting with a lightsaber, the only flash of color, across his lap; a panel of a noir comic wherein a woman holds a shotgun, the scene built of mosaic tiles from what could be DIY band flyers or other advertisements or fragments of the artist's other work; a black-and-white-and-shades-of-gray painting of a couple wearing gas masks in a romantic embrace, the date 05.05.03 underneath. Each other wall plays host to similarly dissimilar art, curated by the owners and staff over many years. Some names I recognize from gallery debuts Zeke insisted I accompany him to when etiquette mandated he accept invitations to social engagements; others hung desperately, perhaps awaiting discovery by a wealthy patron or as a favor from one of the staff.

No doubt, this place exists because of, and for, regulars. Quinn motions for me to follow her through a thick fabric curtain into a labyrinth of back rooms, some storage, most with closed doors. She stops in front of one such door and puts out her hand to stop me as she dips inside and lets the door click immediately behind her. She emerges maybe two minutes later.

"It is done. Morgeaux will stay here until it is safe for her to return to her life—if she *wants* to return to her life. Otherwise she can start over here," she explains, indicating the coffee shop with her hands as we make our way further into the labyrinthine series of rooms.

"Morgeaux?"

Quinn shrugs. "She had a name tag on. Come on," she says, opening another closed door which leads out into the night at the rear of the coffee shop. "We should talk."

⟨ᴥ⟩

"Ezekiel had been searching for us for years, but what he didn't know is that we'd been following him nearly as long," she starts, not mincing words.

I cross my arms over my chest and listen—what else can I do?—and offer no indication that I do or don't believe her, so she goes on.

"The Seeker was meeting someone—as you found out last night—" I raise my eyebrow at the intrusion but she continues without noticing, "—but he didn't need the lead offered by the Crusader to find us. He already had, though he didn't know it at the time."

"The Crusader?"

"Delilah, this is going to take a long time if you keep interrupting," she sighs. "All will be made clear, I promise." I purse my lips and glare. In that moment she sounded a lot like Zeke and I felt a lot like I didn't need to be scolded by some woman who didn't know me. "Anyway, Ezekiel didn't need the lead, but he needed the Crusader to think the deal was legitimate so he would take what Ezekiel offered—so he let the Crusader believe he needed it."

"So this . . . Crusader . . . he gave Zeke a lead to find you, but what did Zeke give him in exchange?"

"An address."

I raise an eyebrow and cock my head slightly to indicate that I expect more.

"He gave the Crusader Ismae the Bloody. Or, rather, where to find her."

"No," I state flatly, shaking my head.

"What?"

"Did I stutter? I said no. That's—that's not possible."

"Listen to your blood, Delilah. A part of you knows I tell the truth."

"No. Zeke was a Keeper, and a loyal one at that. He'd never betray the sect by handing over a Praedari Elder. Not that he'd even know where to *find* Ismae if they came knocking. She was his Usher but their relationship ended there, a long time ago."

"You're half-right," she starts carefully. "He hasn't seen her in a long time, at least since she entered into the Slumber, and I cannot tell you how long before that. But Delilah, Ezekiel died that night and it wasn't the Crusader who killed him."

Every muscle in me tenses as the predator within rouses. This, the truth I've been seeking, the only thing I've thought about since his body became ash, poised on this stranger's lips, about to spill into this moment and be forever gone. Once said it can never be unsaid—like so many things that passed between Zeke and me in our most intimate moments, like so many things uttered into the night since the beginning of time.

"Delilah, I am the one who killed Ezekiel Winter."

17

Before

"**I**N FACT," SHE CONTINUES, "YOUR BELOVED IS here."

I glance around the alley, confirming that we are indeed alone—the Seeker, the Valkyrie, and the raven—before answering. "I assure you she is not."

The corners of the woman's mouth turn up slightly at this. "It is easy to be certain when you only see what is in front of you. Yet she is here—in her way," she explains without explaining. "You will not die alone tonight, Ezekiel."

The woman raises her sword above her head, a feat requiring above-average strength to accomplish, much more to make it appear as effortless as she makes it appear: as if it's made of nothing more than feathers. A light, dim at first but growing in intensity, emanates from its core. A low hum fills my ears and it takes me a moment to realize she speaks, the words filling the night with the cadence of prayer.

"Lo, there do I see my father. Lo, there do I see my mother, and my sisters, and my brothers. Lo, there do I see the line of my people, back to the beginning!"

The humming of the sword fills my ears, the alley, the night, all but drowning out the words the woman chants. From somewhere I hear a drum. I cringe and shield my eyes from the white-hot luminescence the sword emits for fear of being blinded or burned, but in doing so I am able to see shadow-shapes rise from the tar and start to move around us, at once familiar and foreign, comforting and ghastly. As they do, they become more clear in silhouette: men and women, some children. Some move with the grace of dance; others with the grace of battle, swinging large shadow-weapons at one another that meet with the metallic clank of impact that I'm not sure whether I hear or imagine.

I look to the woman for answers, but she appears as if in trance, the color drained from her eyes as if she's becoming the light from her blade. A raven now perches on her shoulder. Everything is black and white.

The woman continues: "Lo, they do call to me. They bid me take my place among them, in the halls of Valhalla where the brave may live forever."

I feel it then, the sting. I do not see her move—indeed, still she stands, eyes open but not seeing, hands clasped around the hilt of her glowing sword, a trail like stardust joining it and my heart. A curious feeling, crumbling to ash, dying, becoming nothing but memory, becoming nothing.

In my Final Moment I think of her, of my beloved—and it all seems so black and white.

18

Now

"LOOKS BETTER, MUCH BETTER," THE DOCTOR CONgratulates himself as he leads Logan through a series of movements testing range of motion. "You won't be running a marathon this month, but you heal quite quickly, my boy. Quite quickly."

He offers Logan a hand off the examining table. As Logan's feet make contact with the stark white tile floor, a woman in a white coat like Doctor Larkin's comes in from an adjoining room. Separating the two, a large observation window which has been darkened to allow for privacy.

"The girl is all ready to be moved. She looks great,

but I've recommended she take it easy for a while as her body adjusts to—" she stops herself short as she notices Logan.

Doctor Larkin waves as if to give her permission to continue. "We're surrounded by vampires, Doctor Amel. Details about our gun-slinging medical marvel won't startle the boy. And I'd say she's fit to run that marathon that this one can't," he jokes, slapping Logan on the back. "Besides, I know you like to hear your own voice."

The woman eyes Logan a moment before continuing, seemingly unaware of Doctor Larkin's jab. "We don't know the long-term ramifications of the partial blood transfusion. She appears quite healthy, but we haven't yet done adequate research into the genetic makeup of vampires, nor into what changes the body undergoes when made into one. Her arrival threw our research timeline out the window since her case was critical and required immediate attention."

"Partial blood transfusion? I thought you guys

were just giving her a taste of the stuff to help her heal?" Logan asks.

"That was our intention, yes—but when she started hemorrhaging we had no choice but to act quickly," the woman explains, grinning as though she'd won the lottery. "Obviously we didn't have her blood on hand, so the transfusion needed to be allogeneic—blood from another donor. Processing the supply from the tanks takes too long and the only blood we had readily available and prepped was that which we were already giving her—vampire blood."

"Why did she hemorrhage?"

The woman shrugs. "Perhaps a reaction to the blood, perhaps a consequence of surgery. In any major surgery it's a possibility, so *that's* not entirely surprising."

"But something was?"

She looks again to Doctor Larkin, who shrugs and returns to scribbling on Logan's chart.

"How should I explain this? Without getting technical, as soon as the transfusion hit 'critical mass'—as soon as the amount of donor blood exceeded the patient's—her body began repairing itself so quickly that we weren't even able to remove the catheters or stitch her up. Her body ejected all foreign objects and within moments her surgical wounds were healed. Charlotte doesn't have a single scar from the procedure, only from the initial injury where we were treating her with smaller quantities of donor blood." She smiles at Logan. "My daughter is about her age and very sick. What we've done here could really help a lot of people," she offers, looking on Charlotte with pride. "I think your friend—girlfriend?" She pauses expectantly.

"Uh, friend," Logan lies about the girl he's never even met, surprised the doctor doesn't know more about the circumstances surrounding their arrival at the ranch, that they didn't know one another prior to arriving and that Charlotte, for all intents and purposes, was just a stranger on a surgical table to him, Kiley, and Hunter—though they did all seem to feel a certain attachment to or protectiveness towards both her and one another as a result of their unconventional situation. They may be the blind leading the blind, but no way were they were going to be the dead leading the dead.

"Well, I think she's going to be fine—better than fine, actually. But just in case, we'll check in on her regularly," the woman promises.

"Check in? She won't be staying here anymore?"

"I see no reason to keep her under such close monitoring. You can access the medical staff via the tablet twenty-four-seven should something happen and we're just minutes away, faster than an ambulance were we on the outside. If you and your friends don't mind helping her take it easy, I see no reason you can't be reunited."

"We will! It'll be nice to, uh, have her back," he promises.

"A bunch of thugs, that pack," the woman offers apologetically. "Most of them here aren't like that, or aren't for long. Victor never intended them to hurt her—or any of you—but some vampires find it difficult to overcome their more, shall we say, *violent* urges. With that pack dealt with, I think I can finally bring my daughter in for her first treatment. If Doctor Larkin thinks we're ready?" She casts this last question his direction and it's met with his trademark shrug.

"What happened to them?" Logan explores, dodging the question he really wants to ask: who would bring someone they love *here*? Does Doctor Amel really think her daughter would be better off here, amongst monsters, than in treatment on the outside?

"Victor had them escorted to the tanks to become involuntary donors. Has he given you the spiel on Project Harvest?"

Logan shakes his head no.

"I'm surprised. This is his baby—actually, all of us involved feel passionately about the cause. You see, most of the donors are just people, like you and me, who volunteered, but a few are other Praedari he's made an example of. I won't ruin his sales pitch, but you asked about that pack. This punishment won't kill them, of course—that's not Victor's leadership style—but while they're left to contemplate the error of their ways, they can at least be useful to the cause," she smiles. "It might be hard to see it now, but he's an innovator, not a monster."

The jury's still out on that one, Logan thinks. He offers a nod of understanding to appease the woman who then busies herself with Charlotte's chart and preparations for her release.

"You're smart," Doctor Larkin says, jarring Logan from his thoughts.

"Huh?"

"You got a lot of information out of her just now, but what are you going to do with it?"

Logan shrugs. "I'm curious, that's all."

"You act as if covert interrogation is the only way to get the answers that you seek. Have you tried just talking to Victor? Or the others? He's not lying when he says that you're guests here. Most of the security measures and isolation *are* for your own safety."

Logan blinks hard at the doctor, unaccustomed to such a moment of clarity in his few interactions with him. His fondness for Victor might be touching were the circumstances different. A sharp knock on the glass interrupts their chat. Made two-way again, a perky girl on a hospital bed waves at Logan and Doctor Larkin through the glass while Doctor Amel talks to her. She's dressed in jeans and an autumn-hued flannel with the sleeves rolled part of the way up, the scar Doctor Amel spoke of probably hidden underneath. Most people look small and frail and helpless after such an ordeal, dwarfed by a hospital gown and decorated in bandages, but Charlotte looks to Logan as rested as if she just returned from a beach retreat far away from this place. *How much does she remember about what happened the night she was brought here?*

Maybe more importantly, what does she remember about being here?

Now

"**I** MUST SAY, I'M SURPRISED YOU WANTED A TOUR," Victor says with a smile.

Hunter shrugs. "I'm getting a little stir-crazy."

"Logan said something to that same effect—I do apologize for the close quarters. I considered rooming you each separately but I thought that, given the sudden *unique* set of circumstances, you'd want some company. And it's easier to keep a single pack on patrol in this sector than it would be to spread out their security detail to include multiple living quarters," he offers.

"Why are you explaining this to me?" Hunter

challenges. "Logan said the doctor told him lots of stuff, too."

Victor chuckles. "As I've said, you're guests here. We don't intend to hide the work we're doing here, we're just not ready to go public quite yet." He pauses. "And, if I'm quite honest, you're four kids surrounded by dozens of vampires. Forgive my confidence in saying that it would take more than your combined talents to bring down a facility that the Keepers haven't even figured out exists."

"Fair," Hunter reflects.

Victor leads him back through the facility much the same way they were brought through that first night, Hunter's mental inventory of gleaming and seamless stainless steel doors reinforced. The halls smell sterile, the white of the walls and the tile nearly blinding. Victor prattles on about the cost of the facility and the benefits package for the salaried mortal staff as though he's giving a tour to investors rather than a captive.

"We are still in the beta phase for the more

interesting parts of the facility, I'm afraid, so I can't give tours of that yet. I suppose I could show you the stables and grounds—the parts of the ranch we've kept mostly as a ranch, if you're interested."

"Which parts are still in the beta phase?" Hunter probes, finding little use in a tour of the outdoors and more in a tour that might give him a *way* outdoors.

"Like the Research and Development Sector."

"What's this facility *for*, exactly?"

"Officially it's a medical research facility."

"And unofficially?"

"Unofficially it's . . . a lot like a blood bank. We subsist on blood and not all of us relish hunting, which requires us to hide our existence from the mortal world. This facility exists to process and store blood provided by donors—the goal is a symbiotic relationship between us and you," he explains with the rehearsed pride of a parent watching a T-ball game. "No more hiding, officially *or* unofficially."

Hunter's mouth opens and closes a couple times as words fail him. *Donors—is that what they're calling us?*

"Not quite what you expected from a bunch of vampires, huh?" Victor beams. "Of course, we aren't without our limitations—as the beta phase has proven. Nor is any large-scale project like this without its political or moral battles."

"Are these the living quarters you mentioned?" Hunter asks, still at a loss for useful follow-up questions that won't betray snark. He gestures to a set of doors Victor hasn't mentioned.

"Some, though mostly unfinished in this sector. We've had to move up our project timeline, so some comforts have fallen to the wayside—like decorating. Others are refrigerated storage for blood. That one's a laundry room." He gestures to a door on the right. "That reminds me, just use the tablet to request laundry services—or anything else you need. Don't be shy."

As if on cue a rather burly-built man pushing a large metal-framed ivory-and-crimson mottled laundry cart, much like the ones hotels use, rounds the corner coming towards them, trailed by a shorter, plumper woman who takes short, quick steps to keep up. She wears bright white Keds that squeak with each step; both wear hospital scrubs. In the cart, sheets, by the looks of it—though the way the man pushes it, his biceps tensed, Hunter suspects there's more than just linens taking up room. Though he barely has time to survey its contents when they shuffle quickly by, both avoiding eye contact, he swears he sees toes poking up from between folds of white before the woman reaches in to adjust the heaping linens.

"Shouldn't they be heading to the laundry room?" Hunter whispers after the two have passed by them a few yards, struggling to keep his voice steady.

"It's burning day; I think they're heading to the incinerator. The thing's a beast, so we don't run it daily. Come on, I'll show you the infirmary—it really is state-of-the-art—then the kitchen, other finished visitor's quarters, and the visitor's parlor, which are in the original ranch house. We dubbed this part the Home Sector," Victor says with a smile, placing a hand firmly on Hunter's shoulder to guide him.

20

Once upon a time . . .

THE RAGE THAT SINGS IN MY BLOOD—AND IN MY
Usher's, and my Usher's Usher's—serves as both
a gift and a curse, the might of our lineage both owed
to it and, sometimes, compromised because of it. Not
just rage, but passion, too, though many never see
this. Still, passion feeds rage just as hunting feeds our
predator within: the latter cannot survive without the
former and neglect can lead to a dangerous loss of
control.

This loss of control may be the thing my lineage
has earned the most infamy for, starting with the
legend of Ismae the Bloody—though it is likely even

her Usher and her Usher's Usher were followed by similar tales of carnage, now lost to time.

◈

Once upon a time—as Zeke would often tell this story to me just before daybreak, after a long night of enduring the traditional ritual torture of our lineage at his hand—once upon a time lived a woman whose beauty rivaled that of Helen of Troy and, in some stories, she was indeed mistaken for her. But this woman lived long before The Face that Launched a Thousand Ships, long before stories could be committed to paper and kept sacred in their detail, long before the Keepers and the Praedari existed as the Keepers and the Praedari.

She lived alone in her immortality, the only Everlasting in her kingdom, betrothed to a wicked man who loved her, truly and desperately, because of what he misunderstood as her own streak of cruelty. He was renowned for his tactical acumen and in time he learned that her own did not disappoint. Together they ruled, though he mostly spoke the echoes of what, because of societal norms, her voice could not, taking her direction on all matters. They allowed no visitors of the Blood, hosted no diplomatic envoys from neighboring kingdoms, and considered the militaristic advances of their neighbors on other domains to be reason enough to remain ever-vigilant, responding to even the slightest misstep with unflinching brute force.

In one story, a woman and her two young children fled the castle walls of a neighboring domain, wherein they had lived as comfortably as could be expected as the family of a well-loved blacksmith, when their home was taken hostage by a neighboring king's soldiers and their depravity. Under the cover of night they fled, and, after many nights, came lost and stumbling—half-starved and sleep deprived—into the kingdom of Ismae (not yet Ismae the Bloody) and her husband-to-be. They were picked up by a guard patrol and brought to the castle.

It was her husband who suggested they put the family to work in their castle forge, being no stranger to hard work, assisting their own blacksmith in exchange for meager room and board. Ismae scoffed at her husband's uncharacteristic softness, rose from her seat beside him and crossed to the center of the chamber to stand behind the kneeling and trembling mother and her two children. In front of their court and guard she bent low near the mother's throat and willed her fangs to slide down, visible to all who paid attention—and all paid rapt attention when the king's lady moved or spoke or even breathed, such was the power of her station and her person—whispering something in her ear.

The woman's eyes grew wide as Ismae sank her fangs into her neck—and wider still when Ismae tore through muscle and flesh and spat a chunk of her to the ground in disgust. The woman clutched her opened throat and slumped to the floor, her own dark blood pooling around her as her children and the rest of the court looked on in horror. She could neither scream nor breath, and no one else dared scream or breathe against the backdrop of soft gurgling and the muffled hysteric weeping of the children.

Ismae took her seat calmly again beside her husband and wiped her mouth with the back of her hand.

"Keep *them* if you must," she said with voice unwavering, gesturing to the children. "But the woman dies."

༄

Here I would ask Zeke *why*. Why would she kill the mother—and only the mother? What was she proving? To whom? Why waste the woman's blood? What happened to the children? Of course, this was long ago and how reliable is a story whispered in the dark for thousands of years?

༄

Her husband finally passed, some say with her help,

and each of his brothers met their end by Ismae's cunning as they tried to claim what was, as they saw, rightfully theirs: their brother's wife and kingdom. Very few outside the arrogance of these men cared what happened to their kingdom for it maintained its isolation for so long that most relegated it to either inferior real estate with an ugly secret or a population so inbred and steeped in backwards customs that they should merely be waited out. Regardless of the reason given, the motivation for their non-involvement was clear: fear.

Neither, of course, were true—and not all dismissed her domain as a blight on the country, though she would have preferred this. Some stories cannot be silenced so easily, however, and Ismae knew it only a matter of time before another Everlasting caught wind of the real reason she endured her tiresome husband as long as she did and protected this kingdom as fiercely as she had.

And a few centuries passed with minimal turmoil, a war here or there, but no true threat to her once-modest kingdom which had now grown to an empire and which she ruled from the shadows, claiming the names of children she never bore—but who would challenge her when none dared enter in the first place? She kept her people happy enough, safe enough, fed enough, and so, few found reason to dissent or leave. Most owned a small parcel of land which was theirs to maintain as they saw fit. Complacency, she had learned, could keep her subjects both loyal and oblivious. From within, Ismae became known as fair, but merciless—if, at the more dire of times, cruel. In reality, few cared how she ruled so long as they could feed their families with the relative freedom her disinterest allotted. Her rules were simple to follow and she mandated no religion above another, allowing most to live unhindered by her existence.

From without, tales spread of a cult dedicated to Ismae. Their purpose and her role in its inception varied wildly between versions, but the gist remained the same: her empire existed under her protection so long as those within remained loyal. To some, she became a savior, having delivered her people from their wicked king after suffering his wrath for their transgressions and protecting them from other wicked men who sought only to conquer. To others, she basked in the attention of her so-called cult as an aspect of the Goddess Aphrodite herself, or an oracle or something like it, gaining power from their worship and holding them captive under a spell or out of fear, to ends unknown. And to others *she* became *they* and they—her supposed mortal bloodline—kept control of their empire by strategy and strength, defending themselves against incursions but not wasting the resources or lives to take what wasn't rightfully hers, no magic or martyrdom required.

Regardless of the form, the fairy tales breached this world and pierced the shadow kingdoms of the Everlasting, most of whom could not rule or live as openly, as boldly, as Ismae and thus were forced to rule by proxy. A few such powerful Everlasting came together to lead a multi-kingdom assault against her empire, out of fear or jealousy, cloaked in the flimsy chivalry of saving her from herself. Looking back, the Keepers would cite the need to hide one's nature from humanity and her open, repeated violations of this law as justification for their assault—as justification for the emergence of their sect. History is written in retrospect, after all.

What no one knew: she anticipated this, having had a vision some centuries prior. What no one knew: this battle would mark the start of the war between the Keepers and the Praedari. What no one knew: Ismae never intended to mother a revolution, only to protect and assert her right to rule, just as every ruler before her.

What no one knew: she didn't just command her and her husband's armies, but trained them and fought alongside them in disguise since before they were betrothed.

What no one knew: to what lengths this woman would go to protect her empire.

So she Ushered the entirety of her army. The

mortal forces of those who rallied against her were met with legions of Everlasting, against whom battle after battle was fought and lost. Still, they persisted, and the war continued for many years, changing shape and purpose and giving her time to amass another mortal army to lie in wait should her Children fall.

In the aftermath, the thing most remembered wasn't that the newly formed Keepers asked Ismae to serve as their warlord, nor that she declined, nor even that she instead turned her army of Everlasting against them. In the aftermath, the thing most remembered wasn't that she fought alongside her army, her Children, the blood of her Blood—but instead, the thing most remembered is how she then turned *herself* against her army, single-handedly destroying the legions of Everlasting she had Ushered and now had no use for; who fought for her, who owed their unlife to her. This is how she earned the moniker "Ismae the Bloody" and the gift-curse of her berserker Bloodline.

There she stands, blood-drenched, bare hands clutching the sloppy entrails of another just like her, one of the

Everlasting. The battlefield now covered in the thick muck of ash and blood and fragments of those fallen but not quite dead, those left encircling her, closing the distance between themselves and their progenitor. In an instant she spins on one who's crept behind her, unaware that though she doesn't see him she needn't see him; in the next his comrade's intestines, still attached to an opened gut, are wrapped once, twice, three times around his throat as she pulls in opposite directions, hard enough in a single tug to choke the breath from a mortal but that's not her objective, that's not good enough, so she keeps pulling. Amazing, the strength of something meant to stay tucked away in this weak fortress of flesh, hidden in our guts. The sinewy muscle cuts into the throat of the man whose hot life-force gushes forth, spraying her but indistinguishable from the blood of hundreds as nameless as he, to whom she lent the Gift of Immortality only to take it again in an instant.

Ismae the Bloody awakens face down in the cooling putrid sludge of ash and blood, alone, and weeps. The predator within slinks, satisfied, to a far corner of her soul and, though she has no recollection of the past few hours, a feeling like molten iron knots in her gut builds up the skeleton of a cage around her heart. She can taste their blood, the metallic choir that sang on her tongue and down her throat. These were the people who were willing to give their lives to protect what she'd built. And they had. After all, the empire could not support so many predators.

At her throat, the Stone of Nyx hangs matte and black, spent.

This story, of course, would be lost to time—were it not for the ravens.

21

Now

ꟼ COME TO WITH QUINN STRADDLING MY CHEST, MY
arms pinned above my head by my wrists. I am
strong and still startled by her strength, her form
seeming to contain more mass than possible by the
laws of physics. The neckline of her top stained with
more blood than before, a sniff confirming that it
is hers—I must have caught her off guard initially,
landing a lunge and tearing into her neck with my
fangs. Not me, but my inner Beast. Of course, no
trace of the wound adorns her throat.

As the haze subsides I realize she speaks to me.

"Have you calmed, Oracle?" Her voice seems to

come from nowhere and everywhere at once, echoing in the empty parking lot and causing my predator within to slink back into the recesses of my psyche.

"Get off me!" I snarl and she does, launching backwards with startling grace and maintaining the readied stance of a warrior a few feet from me.

I stand. She doesn't speak for several moments, her posture relaxing; she looks on me as a mother who hopes she needn't reprimand an errant toddler in the checkout line of the grocery store, coolly and expectantly.

"Tell me. Tell me how you did it. Tell me *why*," I manage to choke out. I cannot say his name. His name rings in my ears with the same rhythm as the blood that has rushed there.

"We don't have to do this now," she offers.

"Tell me!" My shout fills the night, scaring his name from my veins.

"Ezekiel Winter made a choice that night. I merely carried out his wishes."

"Liar!" I snarl again.

"I am a Valkyrie. He could have chosen to join the Honored Dead in Valhalla or he could have chosen to die forgotten. He spent most of his unlife searching for what stood before him in that moment. I won't say his choice was easy, but it was his to make."

"We hail from a line of warriors. The fight is in our blood. *Our* blood! He'd never roll over to die like a dog whose master abandoned him," I spit. "If you are *truly* one of the Valkyries"—a flimsy argument borne of desperation, but I commit nonetheless—"why meddle? Why seek me out? Why—?"

"So the Seeker did share his research with his beloved?" Quinn proposes with a wry smile. "It is true that we rarely meddle in the affairs of others as we prepare for Ragnarok. I sought you out because you have a role in all of this—beyond what you know, beyond what you may ever truly understand. But above all, I promised Ezekiel."

A promise, the sucker punch. My field of vision narrows, blackness tinging the edges and creeping like tendrils to obscure the back of the coffee shop, the parking lot, the woman standing with sword and shield before me as if we stepped out of some History Channel special—Quinn the Valkyrie, Quinn the Murderer, Quinn the Keeper of Secrets, of Promises, of Zeke's Final Moment.

"He—he wouldn't. He wouldn't choose to leave me . . ."

"Delilah, Ezekiel chose to join the Honored Dead in Valhalla, but he didn't leave you. That's why I'm here."

"Take me to him." The words take me by surprise but merely elicit a slow shake of the head from the Valkyrie.

"Do you know what it is you ask?"

I nod.

"His fate is not yours—but you, too, will face a difficult choice when the time comes."

"Enough!" I spin on my heel and start for the back door of the coffee shop only to find Quinn falling quickly in step beside me.

"I can't take you to where Ezekiel is—but I can

take you to where it is you need to go," she offers. I do not slow down. She sighs. "Where are you going?" I stop, turning my head to glare at her.

"The Council of Keepers charged me with discovering Zeke's murderer—which I have—so now I fulfill my obligation to my sect by tying up loose ends." I take a step towards her. "Then I will seek you out. Whether it takes me weeks or decades or centuries, I will drain you of every last drop of your Lifeblood. In your Final Moment I will be the last person you see. My fangs in your neck will be the last thing you feel. You will remember his name and you will remember the choice you weren't given. I will be your Ragnarok."

"You could kill me now and it would be over—but that won't bring him back."

"Vengeance is its own reward. You will die when *I* choose," I snarl, stepping towards her. "Until that moment I will be every creaky stair, every flicker of shadow, the thing that lurks inside you and never lets your inner Beast rest."

I think of the moment I learned he'd died, and the endless stream of moments thereafter.

"Every night you will rise, exhausted, and think of me. Every sunrise you will fight to keep your eyes open so that your dead heart might keep its phantom metronome another moment longer."

Had she merely honored his request? Did it matter? No. Ash is ash.

"You will forget this promise: when you die you will see my face."

And when I die, I will see his. Just as I do every night I rise and every sunrise I return to slumber.

"Live knowing by whose hand your Final Moment will be delivered."

"Be that as it may," she sighs, "your beloved died a good death. And if I die by your hand, I will, too." She falls in step with me again.

"What honor is there in a death you choose?" I challenge, her story of Zeke's Final Moments still not making sense to me. Though I know less of the

Valkyries than Zeke did, I poured over those notes as diligently after his death.

"Where else would honor dwell than in the bloodswell of an enemy?"

"But Zeke didn't view you as an enemy." The truth is, she—they, the Valkyries—might be the one thing he loved that rivaled his love for me. Not who they were, but what.

"You're right. He didn't—and I wish you wouldn't. But every time a warrior enters battle they have decided how they will die. The battle Ezekiel fought that night wasn't by combat; his decision wasn't to die a physical death—nonetheless, he chose to die the moment he gave them Ismae the Bloody. Look, if I explain, everything will be undone. Don't you see, Delilah? Everything unfolds as it must, as long as I do not meddle. You've vowed your revenge and I respect that you will honor that. For now, let me help you. Let me honor the promise I made," she implores.

After

MY JAW ACHED FROM CLENCHING, MY HEART FROM grieving the unknown. Looking back, the fate I wished on Quinn mirrored my own from the moment the news of Zeke's murder reached me until that moment when she confessed to it. Until then I flinched at every car backfiring, poured over shadows of clues that weren't clues at all, chased feelings and hunches as though they might hold the key to unlocking the secret of my beloved's death. In a way, I died every night upon awakening. The truth is, her confession delivered me from that purgatory in which

I lived and relived his Final Moment as though it were my own.

A part of me, even in that moment, was grateful.

Of course, I'd never tell her this—not until I fulfilled my vow to her and brought her to her Final Moment. But that is a story for another time.

23

Now

"I WAS WONDERING WHY I SUDDENLY HAD ACCESS TO your quarters," Lydia says, taking a cross-legged seat on Kiley's bed. The patterned coral bedspread in stark contrast to her rather drab signature style.

Kiley shrugs. "I convinced Victor that if your pack was going to be on security detail you might need it. He didn't seem to want to grant access to that Pierce guy, or John—" she pauses a moment before struggling to continue. "I—I'm sorry. I didn't mean—I just mean—"

Lydia shakes her head and offers a slight wave. "It

is what it is. We're not immortal and he had a good run."

"Had a good run? Lydia, he was your packmate. You guys seemed kinda close, in a weird way, you fought like brother and sister the *entire* drive out here."

"Well, aren't you Ms. Observant?" Lydia retorts.

Kiley shrugs. "I observe. It's what I do. People aren't as interesting as they think they are. When it comes down to it, we have the same impulses, the same fears. The same responses to grief. Like, I see that you didn't sleep," she gestures, indicating Lydia's puffy and red-rimmed eyes. "And I have no doubt that if Victor hadn't granted the three of us sanctuary you'd have bitten Hunter's head off—quite literally—when he asked you about giving him a tour last night."

"I *did* sleep, actually. Sun goes up, vamps go down—no matter what. We can't fight it. But—" she squirms, picking at a loose thread in the torn-out knee of her jeans. "But I guess not well. I mean, I was out, I couldn't move, but I *feel* like I was up all day."

"That's grief," Kiley murmurs.

"Yeah, I guess."

"Tell me about him," Kiley offers.

"What?" Lydia's lip curls up in something like a sneer. "No—really, that's unnecessary. Not much to say—you met him." Her eyes dart to the ceiling, a signal that she's lying which doesn't go unnoticed by Kiley. "I'm fine. It's not the first time I've lost someone I cared about. Pierce either. You can't live almost forever without sweeping up some ash once in a while."

"You know I can't help but conveniently ask who . . ."

Lydia sighs. "Yeah, I know. I guess this is how people bond or whatever."

"You didn't have to come tonight. I actually didn't expect you to."

"Yeah, me either. After last night it's a nice change of pace, having some down time—Victor's taken my pack's security detail so we have time to mourn or whatever."

Kiley's features betray her as she attempts to hide a look of surprise. "Really?"

"Sure," Lydia shrugs. "Most Praedari observe the Rite of Mourning when a packmate ashes. Whether he *wants* to grant us the time or not, he will—to keep up appearances."

"That sounds political. So . . . have you?"

"Not yet. The pack hosts others for the rite and honestly it's the furthest thing from my mind right now."

"What has you distracted?"

"Revenge."

Kiley offers a knowing nod. "It sounds like the rite would provide some closure."

Lydia slumps to her side and stretches out her legs on the bed, grabbing a pillow to prop herself up with. "Aren't you all wise all of a sudden, human."

"I went to parochial school. Catholic parochial school. Most of our curriculum is about death."

"Ashes to ashes, right?" Lydia quips.

"Is that really what happens when you die? You turn to ash like on TV?"

"Yep."

"Have you ever killed anyone?" Kiley asks.

"Sure."

"I mean vampires," Kiley elaborates.

"Sure."

"Why?"

"Lots of reasons," she shrugs as if they're discussing why someone might choose a Nissan over a Ford. "It's frowned upon, though—at least, Praedari do not kill one another. If a Keeper starts with us all bets are off. It's pretty brutal between our factions. 'Survival of the fittest' and all that."

"So you've killed another vampire? A Keeper?" Kiley reaches under her pillow and pulls out her small black journal and a pen.

"You're taking notes? Seriously?"

"You promised me interviews."

"Fine," Lydia sighs. "And I *was* a Keeper. But yes, I've killed them."

"Why?"

"Ugh, Kiley, we could go at this all night," Lydia groans.

"Fine. What about the first time? Who, why?"

"Why are you so fascinated by this?"

"What else have I got to do?"

"I mean, about *my* story. I get why vampires are interesting."

"I'm interested in *who*, not what," Kiley says softly.

Lydia cocks her head to the side a moment before continuing. "I guess I owe you story time. I kidnapped you, after all. So, the one who Ushered me—made me a vampire—she was a Keeper. She was old even then and that was just a few decades ago. Keepers are like—you know what, it doesn't matter. I'd be here all night explaining our screwed-up political system, but soon it won't matter at all."

"How did she make you?"

"You mean, like, biologically, scientifically, step-by-step how did she do it?"

"No, no, no—I change my question: why did she make you? You don't look any older than me."

"Because I'm charming?"

Kiley scowls.

"Rude!" Lydia throws a pillow at Kiley without much force. "Alright, alright—I came to work for her. I'd been bounced around foster homes and living on the street for as long as I could remember and her operation was going to be my last stop."

"What kind of operation?"

"Recruitment. Anyway, she saved me from myself, I guess."

"So you killed the one that made you?"

"What? No. You don't live this long pickin' fights you won't win. She's *scary*—but she made others, too, and we all lived together for a while. I grew really close to another woman who happened to be Temperance's favorite pupil. She was my best friend."

"And you killed her?"

"Seriously, Kiley—will you let me tell the story?" Lydia challenges.

"Sorry. Continue."

"And I killed her."

Kiley blinks at her. "That's it? That's how the story ends? With, 'And then I killed her'?"

"That's how her story ends."

"You *just* said you were close to this girl!"

"There's more to the story, calm down. It's just that it's ancient history, you know? Baudelaire wrote 'Remembering is only a new form of suffering.'"

"Did you seriously just drop Baudelaire in casual conversation?"

Lydia shrugs. "It's like . . . as a child, did you ever lose a pet? I mean, not like the family dog that you grew up with for most of your life, but, like, a hamster or a goldfish that you got and it died a few weeks later?"

"I don't think I'm going to like where this analogy is headed, but yes, a hamster. I had him for six months. His name was Ham-Ham."

"Does talking about Ham-Ham make you sad?"

"Well, no. It was a hamster and I was eight. Dad ran him over with a lawn mower."

"Why was your hamster outside?"

"So not the point here."

"Right. But there you go. He's dead but you've moved on."

"But—no. That's a hamster, not a *person*! And I didn't *kill* him."

"I'll bet he didn't wander outside on his own . . . "

"Again, *so* not the point here!"

"Okay, the metaphor wasn't the greatest but trust me when I say that time really does heal all wounds. Sometimes it just takes *a lot* of time. When Ham-Ham died, did you think you'd ever not be sad?"

"No, I guess not." Kiley considers her next question before asking it, not sure she wants to know the answer but having gone too far not to ask. "So . . . why'd you kill her?"

"Survival leaves no room for sentimentality," Lydia says simply.

"Wow," Kiley says after about a minute of silence. "That was some real talk. I feel like I should share something devastating to even the score. Ham-Ham's about it, though."

"Look, Kiley—it's not like that. I can't really explain it to you, but once you've outlived your expected lifespan, some things just aren't a big deal anymore. Like death. Like dying."

Kiley wants to argue, wants to bring up Johnny while the wound is still fresh because she knows it will get a rise out of Lydia, might even be what she needs to begin putting this behind her, but she doesn't. Instead she leans forward, pausing a moment before throwing her arms around Lydia, pulling her tight against her. She holds on for several moments, channeling into the impromptu embrace all the fear, all the anger, all the uncertainty plaguing her.

When Kiley's grip loosens, Lydia pulls away, blushing, the glisten of tears in her eyes.

"I—I'm sorry. I didn't, I mean . . . " Kiley stammers.

Lydia waves it off. "It was a hug, not a marriage proposal."

Kiley studies her a moment before speaking. "Lydia—why're we here?" She changes the subject.

"I was afraid you'd ask that."

"Above your pay grade?" she jokes, borrowing from their earlier conversation.

"Nah, I was kidding about that. You're here now, it's not really a secret anymore. Remember how I said there were two factions, us—the Praedari—and the Keepers? And that soon they wouldn't matter anymore?"

Kiley nods.

"Well, the plan is to awaken the very first Praedari."

"Awaken?"

"The CliffsNotes version is that she'll awaken and eat the Keepers."

"And us," Kiley says drily, eyes narrowing suspiciously. She hugs a pillow tightly to herself.

"What? No. That would be such a waste of time.

You're like a single Pringle each to her," she teases. "*You're* here because the four of you will help awaken her. You're descendants of the first Praedari."

"No part of me wants to ask this next question: *how* will we help awaken her?"

"You'll donate some blood." Lydia grabs for Kiley's journal, a mischievous smile tugging at the corners of her lips. "So, what'd ya write about me?"

24

GREETINGS CITIZENS OF THE WORLD. WE ARE Anonymous. We are reaching out to you in such a direct manner because we have exhausted every other avenue. The influence of the vampires is far-reaching and inclusive—and the threat very real. The violence transpiring globally has made us as a collective reevaluate our priorities in response to what has become a supernatural epidemic.

On Thursday, October 26 at 11:59 p.m., after multiple mainstream media appearances seem to have caught the attention of the vampires, the blog penned by someone calling himself "Doc" was removed in its entirety. Shortly following, other blogs, vlogs, articles, discussions, and relevant sites were also taken down. This widespread censorship of those standing up to our oppressors must end.

Vampires are among us. What was once considered myth has now become undeniable fact. We are held by a code of honor to protect those who are defenseless, both in the cyberworld and the real world, and to that end we will read a list of organizations in the government, public, and private sectors known to be infected by their ranks, as well as a list of known vampires and their aliases—both within these organizations and without. We will stream photographs of these individuals as they become available, as well as any video submissions of encounters with the vampires that we're able to collect. Any information we glean from you, citizens of the world, about their strengths, weaknesses, powers, abilities, influence, and destruction will only help us in our common mission.

Vampires, consider this a formal hit list.

Citizens, consider this war. Protect yourselves. Arm yourselves. Be vigilant. The longest night has come.

25

Now

"IT'S PROPAGANDA—" BUT BRANTLEY IS INTER-rupted as he leans back in his seat and props his feet up on the large mahogany table that gleams as if a mirror.

"You imbecile! Don't you remember the Inquisition?" Alistair challenges.

"Did you really just play the Inquisition card? I'm saying that this kind of stuff surfaces all the time in the darkest corners of the internet and it never amounts to anything."

"Anonymous has rallied the entire world to take up

pitchforks and grill us with the morning sun. I think it warrants *some* consideration," Evelyn interjects.

"Perhaps if Brantley hadn't poked the bear . . . " Alistair mutters.

"Hey, the Council was squirming because of the amount of legitimate media attention that one conspiracy theorist guy received, so I made him disappear."

"Without the Council's approval," Leland offers, always attentive to decorum and protocol.

"The formation of the Council of Keepers wasn't so we remain stagnated while waiting for a formal vote, thus making us vulnerable to outside threats because of our inaction," Brantley says, letting his feet fall to the floor with a heavy thump and leaning forward. He locks eyes with Leland. "The formation of the Council of Keepers ensures that we take the necessary action to safeguard the tenets on which our sect was founded."

"You dare challenge my reading of the Code of

the Council of Keepers?" Leland snarls as he stands, leaning forward on the table with his clenched fists.

Brantley puts his hands out in front of him, palms showing as if in surrender. He shrugs. "All I'm saying is it's better to seek forgiveness than ask permission."

"So you admit that it was foolish?" Evelyn inquires.

"No. I stand by my decision. I just thought a Bible verse might diffuse the tension. People find the Good Book comforting, right?" Brantley explains with a smirk.

Leland growls.

"We're off topic," Temperance speaks up, directing her words towards Leland who visibly calms in an instant, frowning at the manipulation. "Regardless of who did what, we need to focus on what we can do *now*."

"And has the girl updated you on her progress?" Alistair asks with an edge to his voice.

"Me? I only know as much as the Council, of course," Temperance begins innocently, "but I've invited the Conqueror to give a progress report as her proxy."

As if on cue, Leland opens the doors of their lavish conference room to a waiting Caius and ushers him inside. He gestures to the empty seat but Caius declines.

"I've been summoned and so I've come. What is your need of me?" he asks, voice like gravel.

"We wish merely for a report on Delilah's progress," Temperance speaks out of turn but no Elder dares call her out on it, figuring it best to let beauty handle the beast.

Unaware that Delilah had not kept the Council even minimally updated on her mission—but not at all surprised by this—Caius thinks quickly. "Delilah revisited the location of Zeke's murder and found a witness. She has gone off the grid to pursue the resulting lead, but I expect a call from her by sunrise. Shall we all wait here until the call comes in?" he asks, gambling that the Elders would rather not sit vulnerable in the conference room should the phantom call come in too close to sunrise for them to return to their respective domains. They may be ancient, but none of them could outlive the sun.

Temperance smiles at the strategy. "Of course not, Caius. We will expect your report first thing tomorrow evening, but let us all exercise patience in the meantime," she suggests as she stands to accompany him to the lobby. She links her arm in his before addressing the other Elders of the Council. "I regret I must recuse myself early from Council chambers. There is a matter I must attend of the most trifling sort but alas," she punctuates this with a sigh, "such matters often make themselves more urgent than is convenient."

The others nod as she lets Caius escort her to the lobby. As the doors shut again to the Council chambers—surely so the others can continue discussing the so-called security threat posed by the hacktivist group—she turns to him.

"The girl has not contacted you. You've lost her and she's put you in this precarious position of knowing both not enough and too much—but still you take the heat for her, lie for her. Why?"

"I've no time for this, Siren."

"You scoff when I propose that you love her."

"Because it's ridiculous—you know this as well as I," Caius retorts, his back to her as he heads up the staircase.

"If that were the case, why would I propose it at all?" she calls after him.

Before disappearing up the stairs and into the night, Caius turns to addresses her: "That's a very good question, Siren. But I know that while you may be a great many things, stupid you are not."

26

Now

"**W**HAT DOES IT EVEN MATTER IF THIS WOMAN rises up and eats all the other kind of vampire? If she wipes out half of them, doesn't that *help* our cause?" Kiley argues. "The enemy of my enemy, right?"

"Right. Some ancient vampire goddess lady is going to drink a cup of our blood, lick her lips and say, 'Thanks! That was refreshing! Now I'm off to eat half of the blood-sucking monsters that walk the night!' without so much as looking our way a second time. That's exactly what's going to happen—silly of me to worry!" Hunter rants, pacing.

"I'm saying if what Lydia said is true, this Elder will be distracted—they will *all* be distracted—and we can make a break for it. We can use this if we play our cards right."

"This is a *war* we're talking about, Kiley—a war between the vampires. Here," he thrusts a tablet out at Kiley. A YouTube video embedded in some other site: distorted and blue, and someone wearing a mask. "Anonymous has caught on and they have proof of vampires. They outted them. Out *there* where our families are, where we should be. Apparently someone was blogging about exactly this and got a lot of mainstream media attention—and then his site was taken down."

"How'd you access that?"

"It's Anonymous. They're everywhere. Even the vampires can't stop them."

"Somehow I doubt that . . . " Kiley laments. "Maybe if we can see it we're *meant* to see it."

"So now the vampires fabricate elaborate conspiracy hoaxes to—what? Make us think the outside world knows about them when really they don't? To make us give up on trying to escape because, hey, it's just as bad—worse, even—out there?" He rubs his temples. "You know what? No. I can't even. I can't do this anymore—" He flops down on his bed, a tear escaping from his eye that he brushes quickly away. "It's all so convoluted."

"I'm saying we don't have all the information. Victor, Lydia, the doctor—they've filled in blanks but we really don't know what of it we can trust. We need someone on the outside who *isn't* a vampire to give us some perspective. We need to get a message out," Kiley comforts.

The sound of a throat clearing startles them. In the doorway Logan stands next to an athletically-built blond girl, about their age. Logan glances behind them and gives someone out of Kiley and Hunter's field of vision a wave.

"Sure, Victor, I'll tell her—pie tomorrow," he says, stepping into the doorway and letting it slide closed behind him and the newcomer. "What the eff was that?! He'd have heard everything if I didn't start babbling about Kiley's freakin' pie craving . . . "

"Charlotte?" Kiley asks, stepping towards the two.

"Charlie, please," the girls says, thrusting a hand out in greeting.

Kiley rushes to her and embraces her. "You picked an interesting time to wake up . . . "

27

Now

C—

Heading to nest. Found Z's killer. Cover for me. Update soon.

D

I spend several minutes silent as Quinn drives, holding out as long as I'm able before finally taking the hammer of speech to the tension that has been building. Zeke spent most of his unlife waiting for an opportunity like this; for the sake of his memory I shouldn't squander it.

"So you're a Valkyrie." The statement manages to

sound hostile though I rehearsed my tone in my mind a dozen times before blurting it out.

"And you're the queen of segues," Quinn teases.

"It was a statement, not a question."

"You'd like to know how much of the myth is in fact truth."

"Something like that. I figure you owe me."

"Those of you living solely in this world have a skewed sense of what *balance* means." She keeps her eyes on the road. "All I owe you is this ride."

I glare out the windshield and cross my arms over my chest. The landscape looks familiar, even painted by the hand of night: highway stretching on, dark save for the Jeep's headlights, empty save for the Jeep.

"Fine," she sighs. "The Valkyries are a collective of female-spirited individuals whose purpose is to bear the honored dead to Valhalla to await Ragnarok."

"'Female-spirited?'"

"Not everyone is born into a body that matches their identity," she explains. "Some cultures recognize this—hopefully society will come to accept this, in time—and we do not deny a place to those worthy based on a mismatch of body parts to spirit." She checks her mirrors and that's when I notice that her reflection bears not the decay nor mutilation most Everlasting find themselves cursed with. "Nor are all Valkyries Everlasting," she adds, catching my eye in the side mirror.

"Really?" I gasp before admonishing myself for showing astonishment.

"Sure," she shrugs. "All learn to pass out of this world into Asgard, slipping between the two at will, but that journey brings difficulties no matter the Valkyrie's mortality."

"But you *are* one of the Everlasting . . ."

"You know full well I am. Your predator within responds to mine, just in a different way since I walk two worlds. To yours, I am both threat and kin, familiar and alien. We Valkyries train extensively as we come to accept and prepare for our new role. Some of this is martial training, but a lot of it is . . . how would you say it? Spiritual? I don't think there's a word for it in this world, but our Beast is not so separate from us as yours. Ours must endure this training just as we do and come out of it changed."

"And if it doesn't?"

"Death is not uncommon in the temple, and takes many forms. While the Everlasting find themselves more capable of physically enduring training, the mortals have not this extra battle to wage. The rate of survival is not as skewed in our favor as you may think."

For just a moment this woman, Zeke's murderer, sounds so much like him I have to blink back tears. How many nights did we waste away discussing death and pain and transcendence and our shadow-selves? How many nights did we toil with ritual whip and blade trying to reconcile our dual natures? How many nights did I think would be my last?

"You had wings—were they a trick of the shadows?" I ask, changing the subject.

"Sort of—I mean, I have wings, they're just not here, in this truck, now."

"Then where are they? Do they retract?" I eye what I can see of her shoulder blades but her clothing betrays no slit nor tear from where the wings should have emerged.

"They're in Asgard," she answers but, sensing my confusion, she continues: "Asgard is a *place*, but instead of being a place near here or far from here, it is a place *around* here, encompassing our world—both an aspect of here and its own . . ."

∽∾

But I don't hear her. Instead, the hum of the road beneath us has become a metronome, counting me backwards into memory. The sun has warmed the beige leather seat between us, between me and him, this man who drives us. *Him. Who is he?* my conscious self asks, echoing in memory. Or impression. Reality fades, becomes hazy like when a forest fire rages many miles away but you can still smell it, see it, choke on it—not a vision, but a *something*.

I know I've run my hands through his hair, short and clean, smelling of fresh-cut grass—or outside does, the window rolled down and the breeze blowing through my own. I know I tease him about spending so much time messing up his own hair in a mirror when driving around the country like this would do it for him. I know I've run my hands along those biceps and their farmer's tan, those ribs that I cannot see now. Wiry, but stronger than first glance would let on, the kind of build that comes from working hard, from throwing hay bales and hauling lumber, the kind of handsome you'd expect to see in a movie about someone like him but not in the real thing.

He turns his head to smile at me, his gray-blue eyes matching the pre-storm sky in a way usually only accurate in poorly-written poetry but somehow he transcends this impossibility. Without the forecast to ruin the surprise, the storm would surely have blindsided us, stranded us, soaked us; instead, he takes these curves confidently, too fast, rattling loose tent stakes in the bed of the truck.

"We could have stayed," past-me offers. "I don't want to be the reason we cancel our trip. You've been talking about this for six months."

"We're not canceling—we're re-routing. You wouldn't have been comfortable—storms out here can be pretty intense. Besides, my family has a ranch out here and it's off-season, we'll have the place to ourselves. A fireplace and the love of my life while the storm rolls in."

"You sure are full of surprises, Victor," past-me coos, wrapping a curl around my finger and gazing out over the horizon. Pastures dotted with boulders, mountains. The sky the same blue-gray, but tinged with pink, hinting at sunset.

"You have no idea," he grins.

༄

"Delilah? Delilah, are you okay? What do you see?" I hear Quinn's voice as if through water. She splits her attention between the highway and me, glancing between the two, frowning. "Did you have a vision?"

I shake my head no, groggy, disoriented. Out the window I think I see the pink tinge of sunset but no, just night. *Did I fall asleep?* "How do you know about that, anyway?"

She offers no reply but a shrug.

"Did I fall asleep? How long was I out?"

"You didn't—you were kind of trancey though, murmuring something, like you were having a conversation with someone."

"Quinn, I know where you're taking me. In a few miles we'll pass the sign for a vineyard—but it's been operating only intermittently for years. Shortly after, on the right, there'll be a trailer with dozens of rusted-out classic cars dotting the lawn. The owner has no idea that they're worth money and doesn't care. Then, for a long time we'll see nothing but sky—until we see the ranch."

"And then it's nothing until after the mountains. How do you know all this?"

"I've been here before."

"Okay," she responds, the significance lost on her. For all she knows about me, I'm comforted that there are still things she doesn't: like how I can't remember anything from my mortal life. Well, almost anything.

"I mean when I was alive. A long, long time ago," I clarify, unsure that it's even true.

"Be that as it may, the ranch you speak of is now operated by the Praedari. It's not going to be easy to get you inside."

I want to tuck this memory away in a locked space deep within myself, afraid that it will slip away as so many already have. Still reeling from regaining a piece of myself, I nod. "*What* exactly am I doing inside?"

"I'm your ride. I'll help you inside, but why and what happens after are on you."

"Because Valkyries don't meddle," I mutter, remembering how she plunged a stake through Johnny's heart before disappearing with him. Was he one of her honored dead?

"Exactly!"

"For not meddling you sure meddle a lot."

❧

The rest of the ride is uneventful. I stop her a couple miles short of the ranch, afraid that we're too conspicuous driving so far away from civilization unannounced. We climb out of the Jeep, stashed in a clump of bushes alongside the road, doors slamming shut in unison.

"I can help get you in," she offers.

"With some Valkyrie voodoo?"

"With this," she says, handing me a piece of plastic the size of a credit card. "A key card."

"Why—you know what, never mind."

"Reconnaissance isn't meddling. Besides, just because we don't meddle doesn't mean we don't *want* to meddle. Our vows preclude it, but we still fight the same urges you do. I know who I am rooting for."

Somehow, while I don't doubt her sincerity, I find myself doubting her perception of what urges she must swallow as compared to what urges most of us Everlasting struggle with. Not once has this woman threatened me. Not once has she met my blows—literal or verbal—with her own. Not once has her Beast within raised hackles to meet those of my own.

Saint Quinn, the Valkyrie—my unlikely ally.

I take the keycard.

"Keep the Jeep," I say. "It's a rental and on the Council's tab."

"No need," she says with a wave. "I'll travel through Asgard." She puts her hand out. "Well met, Oracle. May everything unfold as it must."

I clasp her hand. "Until next time, Valkyrie," I promise, alluding to the vow of vengeance I made in what feels like lifetimes ago.

We give a mutual nod of understanding, then part ways. I resist the urge to glance over my shoulder, knowing that I will not see her walking down the winding country road, her dark form diffusing into night. *It is a place encompassing our world, an aspect of here . . .*

28

Now

THE PROBLEM WITH BEING GIVEN THE KEY IS NOT knowing which door it goes to—or, in this case, what I'm walking into *besides* the trenches. From the frying pan and into the fire, except I'm trying to coax the fire into reminding me how it was kindled. The Crusader, Ismae—why would the Praedari wish to awaken Ismae the Bloody? How do they intend to? What does Zeke have to do with all of this? I'm not sure what I'm looking for or what I might find, but I know that if I use the key card someone somewhere might be alerted to my entry, so I stash it in my pocket as a last resort. Going black-ops seems the best bet for now. Besides, I came without the cavalry, so to speak.

The property seems almost surrounded by the rolling peaks, as though they stand sentinel—guarding what is within, perhaps, or protecting the world *from* what is within. The air smells of freshly-dug earth and sweet spices, like clove and cinnamon.

Come on, remember! A basement window that's easy to pry open or a forgotten cellar door, something . . . I slink around the ranch house, illuminated from within in a welcoming way and somehow familiar, in the way that a dark shape at night reminds you of a person hulking in your doorway until you remember the robe hanging on the back of the door—that sense of immediacy gone, replaced with frustration. Every owl's *hoo*, every rustling leaf, every twig cracking under my own foot giving me pause.

My movement triggers a flood light. I hold my breath, but nothing happens. No one comes. I count: one, two, three, four . . . thirty. *Click* and the lights snuff themselves out.

I press myself flatter against the building, crouching as I make my way inefficiently around its perimeter. It's not long before that familiarity gives way to the unfamiliar—surely the house wasn't this massive, this *industrial* all those years ago? Patches of soil betray where the grass has yet to come in. At the rear, oversized silos and sheds seem to be dropped haphazardly, flanking the large complex. New construction, but not so new that debris clutters the property—no, this has been meticulously cared for, its purpose hidden away from prying eyes while the estate itself remains nearly pristine, out in the open to be discovered or overlooked. Perhaps the previous owner—this Victor person?—sold it to one of those commercial agritourism companies that offers visitors a taste of local rural life for a hefty price tag.

Or maybe this hints at what the Praedari have been up to, what's kept them off our radar until recently: hiding something awful out in the open. I shudder, wondering what I might find inside—missiles? Nuclear weapons? Biological weapons? What could be so monstrous within that it warrants such sanctity in presentation?

I don't know how long I've been staring when my gaze drops to a boot planted near my left hand, then up to scan the muscular, husky form to whom it's attached: a living embodiment of the Beast within, were the Beast as beautiful as it is monstrous. Red, wavy hair worn loose, short beard of the same hue, amber eyes reflecting the moonlight in that way all nocturnal creatures' eyes reflect the ambient light, and fangs. Shirtless, I notice elaborate scarification, as if from ritual, adorning his chest and upper arms. Some symbols I recognize as Futhark, the Runic alphabet, though I know not what they mean.

He is not alone. They could be brother and sister, this man and the tall woman beside him who boasts leaner muscle than her companion and no visible, intentional scarification. Still, my eyes trace a jagged scar from her right ear down across her throat to her clavicle—possibly lower, were it not obscured from my vision by a bloodstained tank top. Whatever could leave a scar like that in immortality she could have just as easily not walked away from. She wears the same red hair as the man, done up in a series of braids and knots away from her face, loose and messy. On each a bicep strains against a similarly etched, thick, silver-colored band. They wear the same expression, though she does not show fang. She doesn't need to—her predator within snarls so close to the surface I wonder if she isn't *mostly* Beast. And yet, somehow I missed both of them; my predator within, until now vigilant, has somehow been subdued by the grace and ferocity exuded by these two.

"What have we here?" the woman asks rhetorically, nudging me with her boot. "A pretty little Keeper to play with?"

"Why, I believe so, Sister," the man says, stepping closer and grabbing a handful of my hair and yanking me upward. I growl. "What might she be good for?"

"She *is* pretty," the woman confirms, cupping my jaw in her hand and examining my now-emerged fangs as one might examine a horse at competition.

"Good mortal breeding, too. Strong bone structure. Whatever vampire stock she's from is purer than most. What are you?"

I snarl and try to turn my head. When I find I cannot, I spit, the foam landing just below her right eye. She cups my jaw more tightly. "I oughtta pry these fangs right from your pretty little mouth, you—" she hisses.

"Mina, we should probably bring her to the boss. That's protocol with intruders," the man interrupts.

The woman snarls at her brother, shoving me back into him. He doesn't let go of my hair, catching me as if I weigh nothing.

"Throw her to the wolves."

"Mina—you can't be serious . . ."

"I *said* throw her to the wolves," the woman called Mina says again, slowly, deliberately.

I struggle against the man as he drags me towards one of the silos, Mina not more than a pace behind. As a generator whirs to life, I swear, for just a moment, I hear howling in the distance.